JUDGE AND JURY

A RAIN CITY LEGAL THRILLER

STEPHEN PENNER

INKUBATOR
BOOKS

Published by Inkubator Books
www.inkubatorbooks.com

ISBN (eBook): 978-1-83756-649-5
ISBN (Paperback): 978-1-83756-650-1
ISBN (Hardback): 978-1-83756-651-8

1

The courtroom fell silent as Judge Michael Hawkins took the bench above the crowded chamber.

It was a sentencing hearing on a murder case. On one side of the courtroom was the prosecutor, seated alone at her counsel table, the victim's family taking up several rows of the gallery behind her. On the other side of the courtroom sat the defendant and the defense attorney. Behind the defense table was the defendant's family—a smaller contingent than had turned out for the prosecution, but a respectable turnout given his deed. The two groups were seated on opposite sides of the center aisle, separated like the bride's and groom's families at a wedding.

And in the back of the gallery, several rows behind either family, sat attorney Daniel Raine. He didn't know anyone on either side of the courtroom. But he knew the judge.

"It is the order of this Court," Judge Hawkins announced, "that the defendant should be sentenced to the high end of the sentencing range."

A sob escaped from the middle-aged woman sitting

behind the defendant—his mother, most likely—but the defendant himself didn't react at all.

"Twenty-six years for the crime of murder in the first degree, plus five additional years for the use of a firearm in the commission of the crime."

Thirty-one years. The defendant looked to be in his early twenties. He'd be out after his fiftieth birthday. A bleak future, but still better than the victim's.

Hawkins made a few more pronouncements about the details of the sentence and probation supervision after the prison time was served, and that was the end of the hearing. It was also the end of the Friday afternoon calendar. Hawkins brought down his gavel and adjourned court for the hearing, the day, and the week.

The guards grabbed the defendant to escort him to his jail cell, where he would spend the weekend before he boarded the bus to prison on the other side of the state. His family watched after him, calling out goodbyes and choking back tears.

On the other side of the courtroom, the victim's family spared no tears for the killer, but stifled sobs were audible from their group as well as they filed out of the courtroom, arms around each other and tissues pressed to faces.

The court reporter quickly disappeared to the small office she shared with the bailiff, who lingered only long enough to lock the courtroom door after the gallery had emptied, save for Raine.

Rather than exit into the hallway like everyone else, Raine followed the judge back to his chambers. He had an appointment with the judge, although he didn't know yet what it was about. But when your former law partner and best friend for some ten years asks you to meet him in private, you don't say no. You ask when and where, and you keep the appointment.

The Honorable Michael T. Hawkins was already seated behind his desk, his face serious despite their reunion. He didn't look any older than the last time Raine had seen him, which had admittedly been too long. That was the danger of professional friendships when one of the friends took up a new profession. Hawkins's brown curls were graying at the temples, and his jaw was showing signs of a five o'clock shadow. The jaw was clenched.

"Thanks for coming, Dan," Hawkins said with as much gravity as that phrase could hold. "I need your help."

Raine lowered himself into one of the two leather chairs placed on the other side of Hawkins's desk. "Of course, Mike. Anything for an old friend. What's going on?"

Hawkins pulled a bottle of scotch out of the credenza behind him and poured two shots of the brown liquid. "It's Trevor." Hawkins slid a glass to Raine. "He's gotten himself into some trouble."

"Your kid?" Raine recalled Hawkins's only child. He was several years older than Raine's own boys. He sipped from his glass, then asked, "What kind of trouble?"

"Serious trouble," Hawkins answered. "The kind of trouble that could cost me my job. And maybe cost him his life."

Raine wasn't expecting anything that serious. When Hawkins called him, he thought maybe his old friend needed an endorsement for the next election. When he mentioned his son just then, he thought maybe Trevor got a DUI and needed a lawyer. "His life?"

Hawkins nodded solemnly and took his own sip of whisky. "Yes."

There was a shade of fear in the corners of Hawkins's eyes. Raine had spent years working side by side with Michael Hawkins, but he'd never seen him truly afraid until that moment.

Raine set his glass down. "How can I help? Tell me what's going on, and what I can do to make it right."

"It's complicated," Hawkins answered. "Too complicated for the end of the day on a Friday. Come to my house for dinner tonight. Cindy wants to help explain it all. I told her I was going to ask you for help, and she told me she'd pick up an extra steak at the grocery store. She knew you'd say yes."

Raine wasn't about to turn down a steak dinner. "I don't even know what I'm saying yes to yet."

Hawkins managed to push a weak smile onto his beleaguered expression. "But you are saying yes, right?"

"To you, Cindy, and Trevor?" Raine answered, picking up his glass again and taking a deep drink. "Of course."

2

The Hawkins family home was in the Magnolia neighborhood, a semi-peninsula north of downtown that boasted unobstructed views of cruise ship piers and Seattle's skyline. It was also nearly impossible to get to, with only one road in, and that road was a half-hidden bridge you would drive right past if you didn't know it was there. It was the perfect place for a judge and his family to live, half-secluded from those who might be angered by his rulings. When they were still a team, Raine and Hawkins often fought for the little guy. As a judge, Hawkins often had to send the little guy to prison.

That was the price one paid for upward mobility in the legal field. And the price seemed worth it. Raine couldn't help but question his own career choices as he pulled his aging sedan up to Hawkins's five-bedroom semi-mansion with a circular drive in the front and a pool house in the back. The cobblestone walkway to the house was illuminated by a row of pathway lights, and waiting at the front door was none other than the lady of the house, Cindy Hawkins.

"Dan!" She stepped outside and gave him a suffocating hug. "It is so good to see you again. It's been too long."

She was in her late forties, with casually styled blonde hair, cut at her shoulders and parted on the side. Light makeup touched her features and a simple pearl strand hung from her throat. She had a comfortable beauty to her that offset some of the officiousness that came with Hawkins's position. She herself had held a number of different jobs over the years, none of them similar enough to suggest a coherent career path. Raine didn't know what her latest endeavor was. But she was kind and warm and, by all indications, loved Hawkins dearly. That was enough for Raine to like her.

"It's good to see you too, Cindy," Raine wheezed through the hug.

"Hey there!" Hawkins's voice rang out from within the home. "You better not be making a move on my lady, Danny Boy. I won't hesitate to hold you in contempt."

Raine pulled away from Cindy and leaned into a strong handshake with the other half of his pair of hosts. "I have no more contempt for you than I do for any other judge," Raine joked. "And I swear, she hugged me first."

"Guilty," Cindy confessed with a laugh. She pulled Raine through the doorway. "Come inside, Dan. I'll pour the drinks. We have a lot to talk about."

The interior of the home matched the exterior. Warm, curated, expensive. The living room was filled with soft couches and chairs upholstered in warm fabrics, surrounding a coffee table that looked more art piece than furniture. Framed art adorned the walls on the way to the open-concept kitchen, where a salad was half-prepared on the island and three empty crystal glasses waited in front of a collection of liquor bottles on the counter. The only things out of place were a 'Washington State University' sweatshirt strewn across the back of the farthest chair and a pair of scuffed sneakers by the back door that led from the kitchen to the pool area.

"Is Trevor visiting?" Raine asked, with a nod toward the sweatshirt.

"That's part of the situation," Hawkins answered. "Trevor moved back home."

"Oh," Raine replied as evenly as he could. The last thing he wanted was for his own teenage sons to move back in after college. He loved them, but he didn't want to be their roommate once they were grown. "Is he having dinner with us?"

"No, he's out with his girlfriend," Hawkins answered.

"She's the other part of the situation," Cindy added. "It's gotten very complicated very quickly."

Raine could see from their expressions that was true.

"Is your go-to drink still an Old Fashioned?" Cindy asked, stepping toward the home bar. "The steaks are probably just about done."

"I bet you're right," Hawkins replied to his wife. He opened the door to the pool area. "I'll check the grill. Medium rare, right, Dan?"

"Right," Raine confirmed. "And an Old Fashioned sounds great." It was nice to be known.

A few minutes later, the three of them were seated in the dining room, a more formal chamber off the other side of the kitchen. The drink was excellent, the steak even more so. But Raine was ready to learn why he was there that night.

"Judging by the top-grade beef and top-shelf bourbon," he said, "you weren't exaggerating when you said this was serious. So, Trevor is in a little more trouble than just a speeding ticket, huh?"

"Oh," Cindy laughed nervously, "I wish it were just a speeding ticket."

Hawkins shook his head. "Where do we start?"

"A lot of people suggest starting at the beginning," Raine responded, "but I think sometimes it's best to start at the end. It's good to know what the stakes are. What's really the worst that can happen?"

"Really the worst?" Hawkins thought for a moment. "I get kicked off the bench and lose my law license."

"And Trevor ends up dead in a back alley somewhere," Cindy added, "with two broken legs and a bullet in his skull."

Raine blinked at his hosts, then set his fork down. "Okay, maybe we should start at the beginning after all. What the hell is going on?"

Hawkins sighed. "It all started with a girl."

"A woman," Cindy corrected. "And it started before that. It started when Trevor couldn't find a job and moved back home. He was depressed and in a bad place. A vulnerable place."

"And that's when he met Lydia," Hawkins added.

"Lydia?" Raine repeated the name.

"Lydia Szabo," Hawkins said. "Beautiful, smart, and the daughter of Emil Szabo, leader of one of Seattle's most successful crime families."

Raine frowned in thought for a moment. "I've never heard of the Szabo crime family."

"That's why they're so successful," Hawkins replied.

"They operate a bunch of legitimate businesses across the city, from dry cleaners to day spas, all to cover up and launder the money from their illegal activities. They were doing great, too, until a sloppy employee at one of their businesses violated a handful of city ordinances about toxic chemicals and workplace safety."

"Like how the feds took down Al Capone on tax fraud," Raine said, "when they couldn't prove any of the underlying crimes."

"Except the feds knew Capone was breaking the law," Hawkins answered. "Szabo's criminal activities haven't come to light yet."

Raine considered for a moment. "Then how do you know about them?"

"Trevor," Cindy answered. "And Lydia."

"Trevor felt bad not being able to spend a bunch of money on his new girlfriend," Hawkins expounded. "She was accustomed to a certain level of living. Fancy restaurants, expensive jewelry, that sort of thing. Without a job, Trevor couldn't keep up, but then, through Lydia, Trevor met one of her father's loan sharks, I guess. A few months later, Lydia has everything she wants, but he's deep in debt. And then Szabo gets dragged into court over some OSHA violations that could expose everything."

"A perfect storm," Cindy remarked.

"A perfect storm for what?" Raine asked. "I see the dots. How do they connect?"

"The code violation case got assigned to Mike," Cindy explained.

"That seems like a pretty useful coincidence for him," Raine observed.

"Oh, it was no coincidence." Hawkins laughed darkly.

"The assignments are supposed to be random, but it wouldn't take much to get a clerk to guide a case to a particular judge."

"A bribe?" Raine frowned at the suggestion. "I know the county doesn't pay all that well, but I can't believe a court clerk would accept a bribe."

"It didn't have to be a bribe," Hawkins said. "More like, one of Szabo's lawyers went down to the clerk's office, made a few inquiries about the case, faked some scheduling conflicts to avoid another judge getting it, and complimented the clerk on their outfit. When my name finally came up, suddenly that was the perfect assignment. Classic forum shopping. Don't tell me you haven't done anything like that to get a judge you thought would be better for your client."

"I've never done it in order to blackmail a judge," Raine replied. But he had to concede there were ways short of actual bribery to guide a particular case to a particular judge. If you were a good lawyer. And Szabo had enough money to have very good lawyers.

"Well, however Szabo managed to get the case assigned to me," Hawkins continued, "as soon as it was, one of his thugs accosted me in the courthouse garage and gave me an ultimatum. If I dismiss the case, they forgive everything Trevor owes. If I refuse, they deal with him like anyone else who doesn't pay their debts."

"And his debts are a lot," Cindy added. "Way more than we can pay off for him."

"Even a pair of broken legs won't be enough to settle the bill," Hawkins concluded.

"Does Trevor know?" Raine asked.

"He knows about the debts, of course," Cindy answered. "And what might happen to him."

"Does he know his girlfriend set him up?" Raine inquired.

Cindy frowned at Hawkins, who returned the look. "We're not sure that's what happened," she said. "Lydia seems to genuinely like Trevor. We think he may have gotten himself into trouble without her even knowing."

"What about the blackmail threat?" Raine asked. "Who knows about that?"

"No one," Hawkins answered. "This needs to be handled quickly and discreetly. The longer this drags on, the more it looks like I'm considering their offer."

"So, what are you going to do?" Raine asked.

"We already did it," Cindy answered. "We called you."

Raine smiled. He appreciated the compliment. He told them as much, then said, "What do you think I can do?"

"You were always the more creative one," Hawkins answered. "You'll think of something. Dig up some dirt on Szabo, maybe. Something worse than loan-sharking. Threaten to expose it unless he leaves me and my family alone."

Raine nodded at the suggestions. "What's the timetable on this?"

"As soon as possible," Hawkins answered. "We're hosting a fundraiser next weekend. I need this taken care of before election season really kicks in."

"An election fundraiser?" Raine questioned. "Already?"

"You know how it is, Dan." Hawkins shrugged. "It's not about winning the election. It's about building a big enough war chest that no one dares to run against you."

Raine supposed he had heard that about judicial elections. Lawyers were skittish about running against incumbent judges they might lose to and then have to appear in front of. Still, there was no guarantee against challengers. It was one of the reasons Raine had never been interested in becoming a judge. He didn't want a job he'd have to spend half his time and three quarters of his money trying to keep.

"Aren't you a little worried about hosting a public event with the Szabo family coming after you?" Raine questioned.

"It's not a public event," Hawkins answered. "It's invitation only. And we've hired some off-duty police officers as security. Nothing bad will happen."

Raine nodded. That was a smart move.

"You should come to the fundraiser, Dan," Cindy suggested. "It would be a good chance to meet Lydia in a setting where she doesn't realize you're working for Mike."

Before Raine could accept the invitation and ask if he could bring a date, all attention turned to the sound of the front door opening and a young man's voice shouting, "Mom! Dad! Surprise! Lydia and I are back."

Hawkins raised a hand to his face, and Cindy shook her head at the development, but Raine was glad for it. He could get the remaining details later. He wanted to see how Trevor had grown in the years since he'd last seen him, but he really wanted to meet Lydia Szabo.

A few moments after Trevor's shouted arrival, he and his girlfriend walked into the dining room.

"The show was sold out," Trevor explained their presence with a shrug. "I guess I should have bought tickets in advance."

He still looked a bit like a gangly teenager, despite his several years removed from that age. He was taller than his father, with loose brown curls hanging carefree around his strong jaw and sharp cheekbones. He was a pleasant combination of both of his parents, although Raine supposed his failure to launch and reliance on his parents might lower his stock among the ladies. Then again, he had somehow managed to land the woman standing behind him, Lydia Szabo.

She had round cheekbones, thick lips, and soft eyes, all highlighted by expertly applied makeup. Light blonde hair, thick and lustrous, was cut stylishly at a perfectly curved jaw. Sparkling jewelry and a designer outfit showed off the lightness of her figure and the heft of her wallet—the wallet she expected in her men, apparently. Raine could see why Trevor had fallen so hard for her. And why he had gotten into financial trouble for it.

She focused immediately on Raine. "I don't know you," she observed. She stepped around Trevor and extended a hand. "I'm Lydia. And you are?"

Raine stood up to shake Lydia's hand. "Dan Raine. I'm an old friend of Trevor's dad."

"We used to be law partners," Hawkins added from his seat.

Lydia's eyebrows came together ever so slightly. "You're a lawyer?"

"I am," Raine admitted, before joking, "but don't hold that against me."

Lydia grinned, but didn't laugh. Her eyes were locked on Raine's. "What kind of law do you practice? Are you being hired by the Hawkinses? Is that why you're here when Trevor and I were supposed to be out?"

Raine returned the grin, but only because it was part of his standard poker face. "Judge Hawkins is just an old friend," he insisted. "Sometimes old friends get together over steak and whiskey."

Lydia held Raine's eyes for a few more seconds, then

broke away with a laugh that could only be described as delightful. "Of course. How wonderful. And here we are, Trevor, intruding on these dear old friends and their steak and whiskey." She reached back and grabbed Trevor's hand without looking at him. "Come on, honey. Let's go to your place and try to salvage the evening."

Raine looked askance at Hawkins as the young couple disappeared toward the kitchen and the back door beyond. "His place?"

"Trevor is living in the pool house," Hawkins explained. "Until he can afford a place of his own."

"He's actually turned it into a rather nice apartment," Cindy allowed.

"Lydia helped with that," Hawkins said.

Cindy nodded. "I suppose that's true."

Raine had no trouble believing that. He was still standing, looking after where Lydia and Trevor had exited the dining room. "She's smart, isn't she?"

"Crazy smart," Hawkins confirmed.

Raine nodded, more to himself than to his hosts. "We've got our work cut out for us."

"We sure do," Hawkins agreed.

Raine turned back to his hosts. "I should bring a date to the fundraiser."

3

Raine's estimation of the difficulty of the case increased significantly a couple of days later, on his way to his car after working late again, a common fate of a solo practitioner. The sun had set, the streetlights were on, and Raine's car should have been the only one in the small parking lot behind his building. Instead, there was a second vehicle—a sleek black sedan much nicer than his own. More troubling was the group of men standing outside it, awaiting his arrival.

"Mr. Raine," a low, gravelly voice, with the hint of an accent, cut through the evening drizzle. It came from the man in the middle of the pack. He stepped forward, and Raine could make out some of his features in the dim light. He was older, with lines creasing his face, and a neatly trimmed white beard covering his chin. Gray hair peeked out from under the hat protecting his face from the rain. Deeply set bright eyes shone even in the half-light. "We've been waiting for you."

The 'we' in question included several young men significantly larger than the older gentleman leading them. Several of them were even larger than Raine, which was notable given his own 6'3" frame. A quick scan of the men's hands revealed one handgun and several metal rods. Raine very much regretted leaving his own handgun in his office. A handgun in a desk drawer was useless if you weren't right there to grab it.

"And in the rain," he replied. "My apologies. If I'd known I had guests, I would have come out sooner. How can I be of service to you, fine gentlemen, this dreary evening?"

The old man took a moment to size up Raine. He had perhaps not been expecting a polite, even enthusiastic, response. Raine didn't know whether that was a good thing, but he was pretty sure he would find out in short order.

"My name is Emil Szabo," the old man said after several seconds.

Raine was the opposite of surprised. He had known who the man was from the moment he had stepped into the mist and seen the crowd blocking his car. "Nice to meet you, Mr. Szabo. Please give my regards to Lydia."

To the extent that Szabo's stoic expression could change, it hardened at the mention of his daughter. A nervous energy charged through the men surrounding him, as if they anticipated being released to attack Raine for his audacity of speaking the name of their boss's child.

Szabo took another moment, then pointedly ignored Raine's remark. "It has been brought to my attention that you were recently seen speaking with a certain Judge Michael Hawkins."

Raine had to smile. He appreciated Szabo's ability to phrase it so that Raine couldn't tell if he had been spotted at the courthouse or snitched out by Lydia.

"I understand that you and Judge Hawkins were once business partners," Szabo continued. "I have a great respect for independent businessmen, and I have no desire to interfere with either business relationships or the friendships that sometimes arise from them."

Raine questioned whether Szabo had made any friends from any of his business relationships. Probably not by accosting people after dark with a cabal of armed men. But he held his tongue and let the man talk.

"However, the timing of your meeting with the good judge is troubling to me," Szabo continued. "As I suspect you may now be aware, I too have business dealings with the Hawkins family. I am here tonight to impress upon you that I will not allow any interference with those business dealings."

Szabo paused. Raine deduced that was his cue to acquiesce. He declined to do so. "Well, thank you for coming. As an attorney, all of my business relationships are confidential. I suspect most of yours are as well. May I suggest that we both go about our business and see where things end up?"

Szabo nodded several times. He looked back at his enforcers, still nodding, and said something to them in a language Raine didn't even recognize, let alone understand. He turned back to Raine. "I don't think you understand me, Mr. Raine."

"Oh, I understand you, Mr. Szabo," Raine returned. "I just don't work for you. I don't know if you got your information from your daughter or from someone who was watching Judge Hawkins's courtroom, but I also don't care. Mike Hawkins is like family to me, which means his family is my family. I think you can understand what that means for me. I suspect a man like you puts family before business."

Szabo allowed a dark chuckle. "Business is how you protect your family. Family who get in the way of business don't deserve protection." He half-looked over his shoulder and whistled. "Alexei! Come here, boy."

The 'boy' in question was the largest of the men surrounding Raine. Several inches taller than Raine, with broad shoulders and thick hands. He wore a long trench coat with a hood pulled over his face. He stepped forward and stood next to Szabo.

"This is my firstborn, Alexei," Szabo informed Raine. "Pull back your hood, Alexei."

Alexei did as he was told. Raine could see a large, mottled scar that cut diagonally across the young man's face, and over the mangled socket where his left eye had once been.

"Alexei forgot that his loyalty to family starts with loyalty to the family business," Szabo explained. "I was forced to remind him."

Raine's thoughts once again turned to the handgun sitting uselessly in his desk drawer. "Nice to meet you, Alexei. Seems like you two are close. I mean, now, anyway. After you buried the hatchet... in your face, it looks like."

He took a step back toward the door to his office. From his current position, he couldn't get there and unlock the door before they were on him, but maybe he could take enough unnoticed steps backward to give himself a chance.

"My father is a good man," Alexei Szabo replied. "He is a strong man, and that's what makes a good man."

"Okay, sure," Raine agreed. "So, what was it you wanted me to do exactly? I can see you're a man who means business, Mr. Szabo. I'm sure we can do business too."

That was Raine's plan after all. Uncover enough dirt on

Szabo to blackmail him into not blackmailing Hawkins. That was business, after a sort.

Szabo stepped forward and jabbed a bony finger into Raine's chest repeatedly. It was all Raine could do not to punch the old man in the mouth.

"I want you to stay away from my business, and stay away from my family. I'm not about to let some low-rent ambulance chaser interfere with everything I've built. Just look at my dear son Alexei again. He made a bad decision, and he paid the price. If you make a bad decision, you'll pay an even higher price. Do we understand each other, Mr. Raine?"

Raine understood two things in that moment. He was absolutely going to interfere with Szabo's business against the Hawkins family. And he was going to need to keep it secret until it was too late for Szabo to do anything about it.

"Perfectly, Mr. Szabo," he answered. "We understand each other perfectly."

4

Sawyer Mount frowned at Raine's invitation. "I'm not really into fundraisers. I prefer fighting the system to funding it."

Raine nodded. They were grabbing coffee at the courthouse coffee shop between hearings. He had gotten his usual. Sawyer had yet to order the same drink twice.

"I get that," he replied. "Me too. Maybe not as much as you, but I understand the sentiment. Don't think of it as a fundraiser. Think of it as a date."

They'd been seeing each other for a while by then. Raine had no idea where it was going, but he was enjoying the journey.

Sawyer raised an eyebrow. "That's not really my idea of a date."

"There'll be an open bar," Raine offered.

Sawyer's expression softened at that information. She was dressed in a navy blue pin-stripe suit, with heels the exact same shade of red as her lipstick. Her short blonde hair was tucked behind her ears. "Go on."

"In fact, think of it more as a case than a date," Raine continued his pitch. "Hawkins hired me to dig up some dirt on the guy trying to blackmail him. What could be more fun than blackmailing a blackmailer?"

"I could list ten things right now," Sawyer replied, "but I do like the idea of sleuthing. But if it's a case and not a date, why not take your investigator?"

"Rebecca?" Raine shrugged. "The event is the kind of thing you take a date to. If you and I are together, that's normal. If I'm with my investigator, our target's guard will immediately go up."

"Fair," Sawyer allowed. "Who's that target again?"

"Her name is Lydia Szabo," Raine answered. "Her father runs the operation. He's also the one who threatened me after Lydia told him Hawkins had hired me. Or after one of his goons was watching Hawkins and saw me meet with him in chambers after hours. One or the other."

"Those are pretty different possibilities," Sawyer observed. "She's either in on it, or not."

"That's why she's our target," Raine explained. "We need to figure out whose side she's on."

Sawyer took a drink of her coffee and nodded. "I know whose side she's on."

"Whose?" Raine asked.

"Her own, of course," Sawyer answered. "The real question is, whose interests that aligns with."

———

"NICE DIGS," Sawyer remarked as they pulled up to the Hawkins residence in Raine's car.

The home was bathed in floodlights shining up the stone

walls and the headlights of cars waiting in the drive for the next valet from the service the Hawkinses had hired for the event. A few guests milled about the front lawn, sipping champagne from trays carried by the catering staff who had likewise been retained to make the fundraiser a success. A temporary touch of high society in the otherwise residential neighborhood.

"Yeah," Raine agreed. "It's good to be the judge."

He pulled forward and brought his car to a stop at the valet stand. A pair of young men in white polo shirts and black pants opened the car doors for him and Sawyer. Raine handed the valet his keys and a five-dollar bill. The young man exchanged it for a claim ticket and a, "Thank you, sir." Raine wasn't sure what the going rate for valet tips was in Magnolia, but that five-spot was the only cash in his wallet. Sawyer would have to take care of the tip when they got the car back at the end of the evening.

He walked around the car and joined his companion on the front walk. At the door, a dutiful member of the catering staff was enforcing the guest list, lest someone like Emil Szabo try to crash the party.

"Good evening. Could I have your names, please?" the woman asked when Raine and Sawyer reached the entrance. She had curly blonde hair and held a pen aloft, ready to check off their names.

"Raine, Daniel," he answered.

"One, Plus," Sawyer added with a grin.

The woman laughed politely at the joke, then began flipping through the guest list. She had to turn to the very last page and then check off the last name on the list. "There you are, Mr. Raine. And Ms. One. Welcome to the party."

Raine thanked the woman and followed Sawyer inside. They were almost immediately greeted by one of their hosts.

"Dan! I'm so glad you made it." Cindy emerged from the crowd in the living room. She gave Raine a hug, then stepped back to greet Sawyer. "And this must be the lovely woman you've told us so much about."

Sawyer looked questioningly at Raine, who offered a lopsided smile. She turned back to Cindy. "He didn't tell you a thing about me, did he?"

"Not a word," Cindy confirmed.

Sawyer extended her hand. "Sawyer Mount. I'm a local attorney. I found Dan wandering around the courthouse one day and haven't been able to shake him since then."

"How romantic." Cindy shook Sawyer's hand. "I'll have to tell you sometime about how I met Mike. It's not much better than that."

"Where is Mike?" Raine asked, in part to change the subject from his personal life.

Cindy looked over her shoulder into the house and shrugged. "I'm not entirely sure. Working the crowd, I would guess. Or maybe trying to find Trevor and Lydia. She showed up, and then they disappeared." She turned her attention to Sawyer again. "Do you know about Lydia?"

"I have been briefed," Sawyer responded with a sharp nod.

"Good," Cindy answered. "We really need this entire business behind us. You should talk to Lydia tonight and figure out where she stands."

Raine's mouth set to a thin line. "Oh, I definitely have something I want to talk to Lydia Szabo about."

Cindy looked askance at Raine, but he provided no

further details. Instead, he offered his elbow to his date. "Let's head inside and see what we can find."

Sawyer wrapped her arm through Raine's. "Let's find the bar first," she suggested.

"It's by the entrance to the kitchen." Cindy pointed the way. "If you don't find Trevor and Lydia inside, I would check the pool house out back."

Raine agreed to that suggestion, then he and Sawyer made a beeline to the open bar. Shortly thereafter, drinks in hand, they traversed the kitchen and exited to the backyard. A stone patio extended to a lush green lawn to the right and a kidney-shaped swimming pool to the left. A few guests milled about near the grass, stealing a quick smoke before heading back inside. Raine offered them a nod, then turned toward the pool and the pool house on the far side of the water. The pool itself was illuminated from within, casting an undulating blue glow on the pool house. As they approached, the hypnotic lights distracted momentarily from the hushed argument that was nevertheless audible through the thin walls of the small structure. It was designed to hold pool equipment, not secrets.

"—not how it was supposed to happen," a woman's voice was complaining. Raine thought he recognized it as Lydia's from their brief conversation last week.

"Do you think I'm happy about it?" a man's voice answered. Raine definitely knew that was Trevor. "You think I want to live in my parents' backyard?"

"You seem pretty comfortable here, Trev," Lydia replied. "You've totally moved in. You told me it was temporary, until you found a job. Are you even looking anymore?"

"Well, I'm sorry if my current home isn't up to your stan-dards, Lydia," Trevor returned without answering her question. "Not everyone can live in a fancy mansion like you're used to."

"I told you that sort of stuff doesn't matter to me," Lydia shot back. "You just won't believe me."

"It's one thing to say it," Trevor said, "it's another to actually live it. You're so used to fancy things you don't even know they're fancy."

"Or maybe you should believe me when I tell you how I feel," Lydia replied. "If you'd done that, you wouldn't have borrowed that insane amount of money from my brother and gotten us all into this mess."

"I didn't get us into this mess," Trevor shouted. "I was just trying to impress you. I saw how you always looked down on things that you didn't think were good enough. I didn't want you to look down on me too."

"I never looked down on you," Lydia answered.

"Because you thought I was rich," Trevor complained. "Would you have dated me if you knew from the beginning I didn't have a job and was living in my parents' backyard?"

"You should have told me the truth," Lydia scolded.

"Easy for you to say now," Trevor answered. "If I'd told you the truth when we met, you would have walked right by me."

"Maybe I should have," Lydia returned.

"Well, there's the door," Trevor called back. "No one's stopping you!"

"Fine!" Lydia replied. "But you'll wish you stopped me. You and your whole stupid family. You'll regret this, Trevor Hawkins. You'll all regret everything."

Lydia stormed out of the pool house, utterly failing to dramatically slam the flimsy door shut despite her best effort. It was so sudden and her attention so distracted that

Raine didn't have time to move out of the way before Lydia ran right into his chest.

"Oh!" She looked up. "Mr. Raine! I-I didn't see you there. I—" She spied Sawyer. "I, uh, hello. Oh my gosh, you heard everything, didn't you?"

"We heard enough," Sawyer confirmed with a half-smile.

"Well, that's just fine with me." Lydia shoved her fists on her hips and tossed her hair back. "I won't apologize for standing up for myself. I've had to do that a lot in my life. Self-important men trying to tell me what I can and can't do, just because I'm a woman. But I know how to handle men like that."

"How?" Sawyer asked, as if she wouldn't mind some pointers.

"Information," Lydia answered. "Information they want to keep secret." She pointed at Raine. "Like your client, the oh-so-honorable Judge Hawkins. He should have told the police as soon as my father contacted him. But he didn't. And now it's too late. He looks like he's considering selling his integrity to protect his son. Speaking of whom," she glanced back at the pool house, "Trevor doesn't want anyone to know about his crippling debt to my family. And speaking of them, my father has done so many illegal things, I could ruin his entire life with a single call to the police."

"And your brother?" Raine asked. "I had the pleasure of meeting him the other night."

"Oh, I already know that, Mr. Raine," Lydia replied. She tapped her temple. "Information, remember? And the threat to reveal it. My brother is no different. That same phone call to the police will put him in the same jail cell as our father."

"You might end up in that jail cell yourself if you're not careful," Raine cautioned.

But Lydia shook her head. "I'm not worried about that. It's not about actually sharing the information. It's about them thinking you might. Information is power, Mr. Raine. I'm sure it won't be long before I have something to hold over your head, too."

"Gotta play all the angles," Sawyer admired over Raine's frown at her.

"Exactly," Lydia agreed. "If there's an angle that isn't covered, that's where the shot comes from."

Raine knew he wasn't going to trick Lydia Szabo into revealing anything she didn't want to, and less so would he be able to charm her. But he thought he might be able to bargain with her.

"Let's exchange information, then," he offered. "I need to know more about your father's operations. I'm sure I can offer something in return."

Lydia grinned darkly. "Maybe. But not here. Not now. Too many ears around."

Raine scanned the area. The only other person in the backyard was one of the off-duty cops, walking patrol in his navy blue jumpsuit uniform. Raine waved to the officer as he passed nearby, but the officer didn't wave back. Perhaps if Raine had been a prosecutor.

"What kind of information do you have for me?" Raine asked. "I need something big to get him to leave Judge Hawkins alone."

"Oh, it's big," Lydia assured. "International, even. You'll see."

She glanced around again. "But I need to leave now before Trevor comes chasing after me and I agree to give him another chance." She stepped between Raine and Sawyer on her way back to the house. "I'll find you," she said to Raine before disappearing inside.

Sawyer started to say something about how quickly they had managed to engage their target, but she was interrupted by Trevor bursting out of the pool house, shouting.

"You know what? I'm not done with you! Get back here! I don't care who your father is, you'll pay for—" Trevor stopped when he saw Raine and Sawyer. "Oh." He pulled up short. "Mr. Raine."

"And Ms. Mount," Sawyer introduced herself. "What were you saying just now?"

Trevor clenched his jaw. His cheeks were flushed and his temples sweaty despite the mild evening. "Nothing. Nothing you need to concern yourself with. Which way did Lydia go?"

"Away from you," Raine answered. "That might be a good thing. At least until you two have calmed down."

Trevor stepped forward in an effort to menace Raine. It failed. He was significantly smaller than Raine and had been in fewer conflicts his entire life than Raine had been in just that week. "Don't tell me what to do. You may be my dad's lawyer, but—"

"I'm your dad's friend first, Trevor," Raine interrupted. "That means I'm your friend too. So, listen to a friend when he tells you to give your girlfriend the time and space she needs to calm down. Your dad's fundraiser is neither the time nor the place to work out the problems in your relationship."

"You don't know anything about our relationship," Trevor shot back, staring up at Raine from only inches away. "I'll take care of Lydia. You'll see." And with that, he stormed off toward the house.

"That was ominous," Sawyer remarked, watching after him. "I mean, it would have been if I didn't think Lydia could take him in a fist fight."

"She's definitely a tough one," Raine replied. "Come on, let's go find Hawkins. I want to give him an update. And find out if there's anything I should know before I try to bargain with Lydia for dirt on her dad."

"You really think she'd betray her own father?" Sawyer questioned.

"Like you said," Raine answered. "She's on her own side. The only question is whose interests that aligns with."

"I HAVEN'T SEEN Mike for a while now," Cindy answered when they tracked her down in the living room after failing to find Hawkins anywhere in the house. Anywhere they looked, anyway. Cindy offered a knowing smile. "I bet I know where he is. Follow me."

Cindy led Raine and Sawyer down the hall to the stairway that led to the upper floor of the house. It had been cordoned off by a velvet rope hanging between two portable metal poles.

"Classy," Raine admired as Cindy slid the barrier to one side.

"We run a classy joint here," she joked. "I bet we'll find Mike upstairs. He can't do these all-night events without sneaking away for a few minutes to recharge his social battery."

The upstairs consisted of a hallway with four rooms, two doors on each side. Cindy gave an abbreviated tour as they traversed the corridor.

"That's my office," she pointed to the first door on the left. Then at the door across the hall, "And that's Mike's office." Cindy pointed to the next room. "This is the guest room."

The light from the pool below filled the room with an alluring blue. Raine stepped inside to take in the view of the backyard. "Didn't this used to be Trevor's room?"

"When he was little," Cindy confirmed, "but once he got into high school, he moved into a larger room downstairs."

"Why is he in the pool house now?" Sawyer pointed at the small building visible below. A warm evening breeze pulled a faint scent of chlorine into the guest room through the open window.

Cindy smiled again. "Because we converted his downstairs bedroom into a multimedia room, and because no married couple wants their adult kid in the room across the hall."

Raine could appreciate that second sentiment. The weekends with his two teenagers were the weekends he didn't see much of Sawyer.

"Which leads us to the master bedroom," Cindy gestured to the closed door, "and the master of the house. In his own mind, anyway," she laughed, then knocked on the door. "Mike? Are you in there? Dan needs to talk to you."

That last bit of information seemed to do the trick. The door opened and Hawkins appeared, looking a bit exhausted by the entire evening, but rallying with a pipe of fine-smelling tobacco.

"Sorry," he offered. "Just needed a moment to relax before heading back downstairs to ask strangers for money so I can keep my job."

Raine turned to Sawyer. "That's why I'm never going to run for judge."

"That's probably good," Sawyer answered. "You're a better lawyer than you would be a judge."

Raine wasn't sure if that was a compliment. Before he could decide, Cindy moved the conversation along.

"Dan said he needed to talk to you," she repeated.

"Right." Raine reoriented himself to the purpose of their conversation. "We spoke with Lydia."

"Already?" Hawkins asked. "Great. How did it go? Did you find anything out?"

"I found out that she has plans to ruin everyone, if she feels the need to," Raine answered.

"Including you," Sawyer added.

"Me?" Hawkins lowered his pipe. "How?"

"By telling everyone that her dad started blackmailing you a while ago," Raine answered, "and instead of telling anyone, you're considering selling your ethics to protect your son."

"That's not true," Hawkins protested, but then considered. "I mean, that's not what I'm doing. I hired you to make it go away, not to capitulate. But I could see how it might look like that."

"Especially if she's the first one to expose it," Sawyer said. "She sets the narrative."

Cindy was frowning deeply at the revelation. "Did you at least get some information from her? Something we can use to get her father to leave us alone?"

"She did seem willing to sell out her father," Raine remarked. "And Trevor. And me, if she could find any dirt on me."

"Oh, there's dirt to find," Sawyer chimed in. "She just hasn't started looking yet."

Raine frowned at his girlfriend. "Anyway, I told her I wanted to talk more, but it was a bit awkward just then."

"She and Trevor had just had an argument," Sawyer explained.

Cindy shook her head. "They're always arguing. I wish they would just break up already."

"I wish they'd never started dating in the first place," Hawkins said. "Then none of us would be in this mess." Then, "When are you going to talk with her?"

"I'm not sure," Raine answered. "She said she'd find me."

"Go find her." Hawkins pointed toward the stairs with the stem of his pipe. "The sooner we get this over with the better. We don't need a wild card like Lydia Szabo running around."

Raine agreed with his friend. He and Sawyer headed back downstairs, leaving the Hawkinses to talk among themselves before returning to their party.

"Where do you think she is?" Raine asked.

"At the bar," Sawyer answered, already stepping toward the free drinks. "We should definitely start at the bar."

"I can't have more than one drink," Raine complained. "I'm working."

"Cool," Sawyer answered over her shoulder. "I'm not."

A few minutes later, Sawyer had another drink in her hand and Raine did not. It was probably just as well. Not only was he working, he was driving. And a clear head would be vital for his conversation with Lydia. If they could find her.

"She is definitely not in the living room," Sawyer declared after a scan of the room.

"Not the kitchen either," Raine added with a glance at the adjoining room. "Split up and find her?"

"Split up?" Sawyer laughed. "We're not teenagers solving a ghost mystery. And anyway, you're going to need a witness for any conversation you have with that woman. The most dangerous information against you is false information you can't disprove."

Raine could hardly disagree. "Let's start with that multimedia room Cindy mentioned."

"You think she might be down there?"

"Not really," Raine admitted, "but I want to see their setup. I bet it's awesome."

The multimedia room was, in fact, awesome. And Lydia was, in fact, not downstairs. Raine and Sawyer spent the next half hour searching the home and grounds for her, but with no luck. There was also no sign of Trevor, Hawkins, Cindy, or anyone else they knew, save two or three lawyers they knew by face if not name from the courthouse.

"Maybe we should ask the off-duty cops," Raine suggested. They were standing outside on the front drive. A few guests were making their way to the valet stand. The evening was beginning to end. "They might have seen where Lydia went."

"You can talk to them if you want," Sawyer shook her head, "but not me. I don't talk to cops unless they're on the witness stand and I'm cross-examining them."

Raine could appreciate the sentiment, but his experience with police hadn't been all bad. Sawyer only did criminal defense work. Raine handled everything. Cops could be useful, helpful even, under the right circumstances.

But before he could say as much, the night was cleaved

by the sound of a gunshot. The sound was unmistakable, in part because it was so close. Inside the house. Upstairs.

Raine sprinted inside, Sawyer on his heels. He threw the velvet rope to the floor and bounded up the steps, two at a time. Sawyer was right behind him, and behind her were a handful of other guests who were either too heroic or too curious to stay downstairs.

The only room with a light on was Hawkins's study. Raine ran to it but stopped short in the doorway. Sawyer slammed into him, sending him stumbling just inside. The doorway then filled with other witnesses. 'Witnesses' because it was a crime scene.

The smell of gunpowder filled the study. On the floor, lying in a pool of rapidly expanding blood from the gunshot wound in the middle of her forehead, was Lydia Szabo.

And standing over her, holding a handgun that Raine knew would match the bullet the medical examiner pulled out of Lydia's skull at autopsy, stood The Honorable Judge Michael Hawkins.

5

"It's not what it looks like!" Hawkins shouted.

Raine was glad to hear that. Because it looked an awful lot like Hawkins had just murdered Lydia Szabo.

"Good," Raine responded. He took a tentative step toward Hawkins, hand outstretched. "Now put the gun down, Mike. Nice and slow. Keep it out of the blood. Then take three steps back and raise your hands."

Hawkins hesitated. His eyes were wide and wild. He looked down at the gun in his hand, then at the dead woman at his feet, then back at Raine.

But before he could say anything more, Cindy and Trevor pushed their way to the front of the crowd.

"Lydia!" Trevor shouted.

"Mike!" Cindy followed with a shriek of her own.

Raine had to take his attention off Hawkins—the man with the loaded handgun—long enough to wrap his arms around Trevor before he got to Lydia. There was no saving her at that point. They needed to preserve the crime scene.

Even if Hawkins had done it. But especially if he hadn't. Although Raine was having trouble imagining how that latter option could possibly be true.

Raine held Trevor for the several seconds it took the young man to stop struggling and go limp from physical exertion and emotional shock. Raine pushed Trevor toward his mother and returned his attention to Hawkins. The gun was on the floor, and Hawkins had taken three steps back as instructed. He raised his hands. "I didn't do it, Dan. I swear I didn't do it."

Any further discussion of the situation was terminated by the arrival of those off-duty police officers who had been hired to patrol the perimeter. They smashed through the crowd at the door and tackled Hawkins to the floor.

In a few short moments, Hawkins was handcuffed, and everyone else, including Raine, was shoved out of the room and down the stairs. Trevor was still calling out Lydia's name. Cindy was calling out her husband's. Sawyer stood by, but bit her tongue as the officers manhandled everyone. And Raine was trying to explain that he was Hawkins's lawyer. The cops weren't arguing the point; they just didn't care.

"This is a murder scene, counselor," the burlier of the two officers said, placing a heavy hand on Raine's chest.

"You can talk to your client after we book him into the jail," the other officer said. "He's definitely going to need a lawyer."

MURDER SCENES TOOK FOREVER to process. The off-duty cops were just the first of several waves of law enforcement that would wash over the Hawkins residence until the wee hours of the morning. They told everyone to stay until the detective arrived, and stood guard at the bottom of the stairs to make sure no one went into the study, or contacted Hawkins, whom they held in the hallway until back-up arrived. It did in short order, in the form of a dozen on-duty patrol officers. They stuffed Hawkins into the back of a patrol car and wrapped crime scene tape around the entire property.

Anyone who heard the gunshot was a witness, and no witnesses were supposed to leave until they provided a statement and were excused by the detective. The hired help who didn't see anything would get to leave first, after each of them wrote a two-sentence witness statement that amounted to, 'Heard gunshot. Saw nothing.' The guests who were inside but stayed downstairs would be next. Then, the guests who had gone upstairs and peered through the door at Hawkins standing over Lydia. And finally, the suspect's family: Cindy and Trevor.

Raine was unique. He was both a witness and the suspect's lawyer. The cops would want to question him, and he would tell them to pound sand. They all knew that, so he had to wait until the very end. But Sawyer wasn't about to sit on a cement porch the entire night.

"Like I said, I don't talk to cops," she announced, already walking backwards away from the house. "I'm outta here."

"You can't just leave," Raine protested. "No one is allowed to leave."

Sawyer stopped and laughed. "Aren't you a lawyer? There's two things you and I both know. One, cops can't actually detain a witness. Everyone who stays here does so because they think they have to, but we know cops can't physically stop someone from leaving without having reasonable suspicion the person committed a crime."

Raine supposed that was true. "What's the other thing?" he asked.

"That even if I did stay, I'm not saying anything to them anyway," Sawyer answered. "So, it doesn't matter if I leave now. You? You're the suspect's lawyer. It would look shady if you left. But me? I'm nothing. I'm the wind. And I'm gone."

Raine shook his head and grinned.

"There's a spot near the hedges they aren't patrolling." Sawyer looked out over the lawn. "I'll see you later, Dan. Don't wait up."

Waiting up was exactly what Raine would be doing, but he wished her well anyway. He sat down on the front stoop, the cement growing increasingly cold throughout the night. One officer checked in long enough to get his name, but otherwise he sat alone for hours, his brain trying to make sense of what his eyes had seen.

Finally, as the sun was beginning to rise over the row of houses across the street, the detective walked out onto the porch. "Mr. Raine. Thank you for your patience. I'm Detective Ewing. I know it's been a long night."

"He didn't do it," Raine cut right to the chase, without even looking up at the detective. It was a mix of a lawyer's advocacy and a witness's observation. "He said he didn't do it."

The detective sat down next to him. He was a man of about the same age as Raine. He looked as tired as Raine felt, with puffy eyes and gray stubble. Silver strands streaked brown hair that he wore slicked straight back, exposing a receding hairline. "Everybody says they didn't do it. If that's all it took, I wouldn't have a job. Neither would you, I'd wager."

Raine supposed that was true, but he didn't concede the

point. "You may not believe him, Detective, but you don't know him. I do. He's my friend. I have to believe him. And that's important."

"Oh yeah?" Ewing cocked his head at Raine. "Why?"

"Because," Raine explained, "if he didn't do it, then someone else did."

6

The visiting room at the King County Jail was illuminated a bit too brightly by the buzzing fluorescent lights overhead. Raine squinted against the light reflecting off the white cinderblock walls. A headache began budding behind his eyes after his sleepless night. He guessed Hawkins probably hadn't slept either.

Raine and Hawkins had been in similar visiting booths together in years past, when they were still partners and worked cases together. But they had never been on opposite sides of the glass separating attorney from client. If it was ever going to come to that, Raine would have guessed he would have been the one in the red jail scrubs, not Hawkins. Raine had bent the law on more than one occasion in service of his clients, but Hawkins was the safe, reliable planner who avoided risks and followed the rules. It didn't make sense that he would snap and murder someone in a house full of witnesses. That meant it did make sense that he was telling the truth when he told Raine he didn't do it.

Raine sat down at the partition and waited for his friend

to be escorted into the other half of the visiting booth. He didn't have to wait long. And Hawkins had definitely been up all night.

Hawkins walked slowly to the seat opposite Raine as the guard closed the door behind him. His hair was disheveled, and stubble covered his face. Dark bags hung under his eyes, but he managed a tired smile as he sat down.

"Fancy meeting you here," he quipped, but the brave smile slipped. "I didn't do it, Dan. I didn't murder Lydia. You have to believe me."

Raine leaned forward. "Despite what I saw—what everyone saw—I do believe you."

"Thank God," Hawkins exhaled.

"But a dozen people are going to testify they saw you standing over the victim, smoking gun in your hand, while her blood was still spilling out," Raine continued. "If you didn't pull the trigger, then what really happened?"

It was the most important question of the case.

"I don't know," Hawkins answered.

Raine shook his head. "You're going to have to do better than that. Tell me how you ended up standing over Lydia with a gun in your hand."

Hawkins sighed. "Okay. I was upstairs, in our bedroom. I needed one more pipe bowl before the goodbyes started. That's when you really have to lean on anyone who hasn't donated yet, and I hate that part of this job."

"You may not have to worry about that job for long, Mike," Raine said. "Convicted murderers can't be judges."

"I know," Hawkins said. "That's why I can't be convicted."

"That's one of the reasons," Raine replied. "How long were you up there?"

Hawkins shrugged. "I'm not sure. Five minutes? Ten? Probably not longer than that."

"Any witnesses?" Raine hoped. "Was Cindy with you?"

Hawkins shook his head. "No. I was alone. I'm not sure where Cindy was. Probably looking for you. We both wanted to know if you ever talked to Lydia."

"I didn't," Raine advised. "She was busy being shot to death."

"Not funny, Dan," Hawkins protested.

Raine ignored the critique. "So, what happened next? Did you go into your study? Was Lydia there? Was she still alive then?"

"No, I was in my room when I heard the gunshot," Hawkins answered.

"What did you do then?"

"I dropped my pipe on my dresser and ran into the study," Hawkins answered. "Just like everybody else did. But I was just closer, so I got there first. Lydia was on the floor, already shot, and the gun was lying next to her. I didn't know if the killer was still in the room, so I picked up the gun to make it safe. And that's when you and everyone else rushed in."

Raine leaned back in his chair and put a hand to his chin. "That's not the best alibi story," he appraised, "but I can work with it."

"It's the truth," Hawkins insisted.

"That should help," Raine replied. He tapped a finger against his lips. "Let's slow it down. Tell me exactly what you saw when you walked in the room and found Lydia on the floor."

But Hawkins shook his head again. "I don't want to do

this. I'm not some unsophisticated client who lost his head in a drunken bar fight. I didn't touch anything except the gun, and I put that down exactly where I picked it up from. The crime scene photos will show the room exactly how it was when I walked in."

Raine knew he was going to need to get Hawkins to talk in more detail about what he saw before everyone else crashed into the room, but he also knew they were both exhausted and there would be time later. After Hawkins was charged with murder. Because he was definitely going to be charged with murder. They both knew that.

"Is there anything else you can think of right now?" Raine asked. "Like you said, you're sophisticated. You've dealt with murder cases as a lawyer and a judge. You know what the evidence usually is on this type of case, and you know what's important. Give me something to work with. Did you notice anything that might help us?"

Hawkins frowned and looked up at the ceiling. Then he dropped his gaze and pointed at Raine. "The window! The window was open... I think."

"You think?" Raine questioned.

"I'm pretty sure," Hawkins qualified, the frown returning slightly. "It was warm in the house with all those people. I remember that. And it's always warmer upstairs because heat rises, right? But when I ran into my study, it seemed cooler somehow. I think the window was open."

"Did you see that it was open?" Raine asked. "Or are you just guessing from the temperature?"

Hawkins thought for a moment. "I didn't look at the window specifically, but I think I could also hear outside. Just the rush of the night air. I'm pretty sure it was open. The real killer probably jumped out the window. That's helpful, right?"

Raine frowned himself. "Only if we can prove it. No one's going to take your word for it."

"Cindy might have noticed," Hawkins suggested. "Or Trevor."

Raine let his shoulders drop. "That brings me to an even more difficult issue."

"What's that?" Hawkins asked with a sudden frown.

Raine knew his friend was already cracking under the strain of the situation. His old law partner should have seen the issue immediately.

"If you didn't kill Lydia, somebody else did," Raine answered. "And Trevor is the most likely suspect."

Hawkins blinked at Raine several times, then squeezed his eyes shut. "Damn it."

"Exactly," Raine agreed. "Even if you win the case, you may still lose it—as a father, at least."

Hawkins opened his eyes and shook his head. "No. No, it couldn't be Trevor."

"Why not?"

"He's too much of a coward," Hawkins answered. "I hate to say it, but I just don't think he's got the guts to do anything like this."

"I like that argument," Raine smiled slightly, "but people do things when they get emotional. I saw Trevor and Lydia arguing earlier in the evening. Was that your gun?"

Hawkins nodded. "Yes."

"Where did you keep it?"

"Top drawer of my desk," Hawkins answered. "In my study."

Raine frowned again. "Not in a gun safe?"

"I have another one in our gun safe," Hawkins answered, "but what's the use of a gun you can't get to when you suddenly need it? You know what we do for a living. You know what kind of people we deal with. It's even worse when you're a judge. I haven't even been a judge all that long, and I've already sent dozens of people to prison. Some of them are already out, and the ones who aren't have family and friends who blame me for what happened to them."

Raine understood the logic. "Who knew the gun was there?"

Hawkins shrugged. "Cindy, of course. Trevor, too. I'm not sure who else."

"What about the people you hired to work the fundraiser?" Raine asked. "Did you tell any of them?"

"The cops asked about any weapons in the house," Hawkins answered, "but we didn't tell anyone else. The caterers and valets weren't supposed to go upstairs, so they didn't need to know about a gun in my desk drawer."

That all made sense to Raine. "Anyone else?"

"Maybe our cleaning lady?" Hawkins offered with a weak grin.

"Let's hope your cleaning lady was on the guest list," Raine deadpanned. "Otherwise, we're back to Trevor."

"Trevor," Hawkins repeated, "or anyone he told about the gun. He's not exactly good at keeping secrets."

"I like that," Raine agreed. "He probably told Lydia. And Lydia probably told her family."

"Yes," Hawkins agreed. "I'd much rather accuse Lydia's family than my own."

"I would too," Raine concurred with a grin. "So, let's do that."

Hawkins managed another weak smile. "I can't think of

anyone I'd rather have defending me than you, Dan. I didn't think I'd have to hire you for two different cases."

Raine shook his head. "Don't worry, Mike. I'm pretty sure this is all the same case."

7

The felony arraignments in King County Superior Court were held every afternoon at 1:00 p.m. That gave the prosecutors time to review the reports in the morning for all of the new crimes that had been committed the night before. Like the murder of Lydia Szabo.

Raine arrived at 12:50 p.m. There wasn't much reason to show up earlier. Hawkins was still in custody and had undoubtedly already been transported to the holding cells behind the courtroom, along with all of the other soon-to-be accused criminals. Raine wondered whether any of them might recognize Hawkins as the judge who sentenced them for whatever their last crime was. He hoped not. He doubted it, as well. Hawkins's appearance was already a lot more haggard than it ever would have been when he was on the bench, and red jail jammies offered a substantially different look than a black robe.

The front of the courtroom was filling up with the collection of prosecutors and defense attorneys who had hearings that afternoon. There were far fewer prosecutors in total.

Most of the arraignments would be handled by the junior prosecutor already standing at the bar with a stack of the afternoon's files. It was his job to conduct almost all of the arraignments, every day from 1:00 to 5:00 p.m., until it was finally his turn to move on and be assigned to an actual trial team. The only exceptions were the cases with the most serious charges, like murder. Those arraignments would be conducted by the senior prosecutor who handled the case from charging to verdict. Whoever arrived to arraign Michael Hawkins that overcast afternoon would be the same prosecutor Raine would be dueling in front of a jury a few months later.

The defense bar, on the other hand, was well represented. A dozen public defenders, of various levels of experience and skill, milled about the increasingly crowded courtroom. They were joined by a handful of private defense attorneys. Most accused felons couldn't afford private attorneys, but the few who could usually made the choice to hire one. Hawkins had hired Raine.

The final group of attendees were seated in the gallery, on the other side of secure bulletproof glass designed to protect the judge and hold the defendants. The gallery was usually sparsely populated, half-filled only with family members wondering what was going to happen to their loved one who had been arrested the night before. That day, however, those usual attendees were joined by a row of cameras and news reporters lined up against the back wall. Raine knew they were there for Hawkins.

Raine looked around the fore of the courtroom again to see if he recognized anyone who might be there to handle the biggest case the courthouse had seen in recent memory. Raine knew immediately who his opponent was: the man who had just walked in, exactly two minutes before the judge was scheduled to take the bench.

John Alexander, Senior Deputy Prosecuting Attorney and Chief of the Homicide Unit. Not Jonathan, not Johnny, definitely not Jack. But his first name didn't matter. Everyone called him Alexander. Alexander the Great.

He was in his mid-fifties and took good care of himself, as befitted a career in the public eye. He was clean-shaven with salt-and-pepper hair that always looked like he had come straight from the barbershop. A dark gray suit was wrapped around a strong chest and thin waist. White shirt, plum tie, black shoes, gold wire-rimmed glasses. A class ring on his right hand and a wedding band on the left. He walked straight to Raine. He could deduce who his opponent was, as well.

"Mr. Raine," Alexander greeted him with a firm hand-shake. "I assume you're here for Judge Hawkins?"

Raine had to smile. A lesser prosecutor would have said '*Mister* Hawkins,' a suggestion that Hawkins was no longer entitled to the honorific he had earned, or that he would soon lose it. But Alexander was the pinnacle of class. He won his cases through hard work and exceptional advocacy, not trash talk. Juries loved him.

Raine was in trouble.

"I am," Raine confirmed. "Any chance you're going to hold off charging him pending further investigation? You can't believe a sitting judge would really murder someone at his own fundraiser with a house full of witnesses."

"I believe what the evidence shows me," Alexander answered. "The victim was shot to death in Judge Hawkins's home, with Judge Hawkins's handgun, and Judge Hawkins was found standing over her body with the murder weapon in his hand. Preliminary investigations already suggest he was being pressured, perhaps even threatened, by the victim's family. That's motive to go along with means and opportunity. I expect the case against him will only get better as we prepare for trial."

Raine was worried about that too.

"So, no, I will not be delaying the filing of charges." Alexander reached into the single case file he had brought with him and extracted papers to hand to Raine. "Here is the criminal complaint. One count of murder in the first degree, with a firearm sentencing enhancement."

"Twenty-five years minimum," Raine said as he accepted the documents. "That's a lot of time for a crime he didn't commit."

"It would be," Alexander answered. "We can agree on that."

"Can we agree on bail, too?" Raine tried. "I know it's a murder charge, but he's a sitting judge. He's not going anywhere. If we both recommend a personal recognizance release, the judge will go along with that, despite the charge."

Alexander blinked at Raine several times. "You honestly think I would recommend a P.R. release on a murder one case?"

"I think you could," Raine answered, "and should. He's a judge. He didn't do this. If you can't hold off charging him, at least hold off jailing him. Your case isn't as solid as you think it is."

"Why do you say that?" Alexander questioned.

"Because he's innocent," Raine answered. "Which means you're wrong."

Alexander pursed his lips together. "I will be recommending a bail of one million dollars, the same amount I would ask for on any charge of murder in the first degree. I will not treat Judge Hawkins differently from any other defendant, better or worse."

"I suppose I can appreciate that," Raine returned. "Well then, may the best lawyer win."

But Raine didn't mean that. Everyone in that courtroom would have tapped Alexander as the better lawyer. Still, Raine was determined to beat him anyway. Somehow.

Alexander nodded at Raine's comment, then strode to that junior prosecutor at the bar to inform him that he would be going first when the judge came out. His timing was impeccable.

"All rise!" the bailiff called out then. "The King County Superior Court is now in session, The Honorable Yvonne Pereidas presiding."

Almost everyone was already standing. There were only four chairs for twenty-some attorneys, and the two jail guards at the entrance to the holding cells would definitely be standing the entire afternoon.

Judge Pereidas sat down on the bench and offered a "You may be seated," more out of politeness than feasibility. She was in her fifties, like the majority of judges, with thick black curls pulled back in a loose ponytail. She had medium-toned skin and dark eyes. She looked down at the room through thick glasses. "Are there any matters ready?"

"The matter of *The State of Washington versus Michael Hawkins* is ready, Your Honor," Alexander announced. One of the jail guards opened the door to the holding cells and called for Hawkins. Alexander gave a copy of the complaint to the bailiff. The bailiff handed it up to the judge. And Raine walked forward, taking his spot at the defense attorney's position just as his client was brought into the court-room by a third, burly and armed jail guard.

Hawkins frowned past Raine at their opponent. "Alexander the Great," he whispered. "That's not good."

"It just means they're scared," Raine tried to sound confident. "They wouldn't put him on it if they thought it was an easy case."

Hawkins managed a slight grin. "Nice spin. I knew I hired the right lawyer."

"Are the parties ready to proceed with the arraignment?" Judge Pereidas interrupted.

"The State is ready, Your Honor," Alexander replied before entering his appearance for the record. "John Alexander, on behalf of the State of Washington."

"The defense is ready as well, Your Honor," Raine answered next. "Daniel Raine, appearing on behalf of Michael Hawkins."

"Thank you, counsel," Judge Pereidas responded. Then, after a moment's more consideration and an uncomfortable frown, she nodded to the defendant. "Judge Hawkins."

Hawkins returned the nod. "Your Honor."

Raine allowed himself to think he might get that personal recognizance release after all.

The daily arraignment court was usually filled with a low hum of chatter at all times, its volume rising and falling, but never ceasing, depending on whether the judge was on the bench and whether any lawyers were actively addressing the Court. At that moment, however, the only sound in the packed courtroom was the judge's voice as she turned back to the prosecutor and invited, "Please conduct the arraignment, Mr. Alexander."

"Thank you, Your Honor." Alexander nodded up to the judge. "The State is charging the defendant, Michael Hawkins, with one count of murder in the first degree, for the premeditated, intentional, and unlawful killing of Lydia Szabo. Further, the State is adding a special sentencing enhancement for the use of a firearm during the commission of the crime, adding five years to the standard sentence. We would ask the defense to acknowledge receipt of the complaint, waive further formal reading of the charges, and enter a plea."

All eyes turned then to Raine. He raised his copy of the complaint slightly. "The defense acknowledges receipt of the complaint. We waive formal reading of the charges. And we ask the Court to enter a plea of absolutely not guilty to the charge of murder in the first degree."

Pereidas frowned slightly. "A plea of not guilty will be entered."

There was one more formality before they reached the part of the proceedings that truly mattered. "I will now review the declaration for determination of probable cause," Judge Pereidas announced.

The declaration for determination of probable cause was a summary of the police reports and, more specifically, the evidence against the defendant. The judge would review it to determine whether there was 'probable cause' for the charge, a famously low standard. The judge was supposed to assume the truth of the State's evidence, draw any and all reasonable inferences in favor of the State, and decide whether any jury could possibly find the defendant had committed the crime charged.

"Any chance she doesn't find probable cause?" Hawkins asked Raine hopefully.

"You were standing over her with the murder weapon in your hand," Raine whispered back. "No chance at all."

Hawkins should have known that, of course, but hope sprang eternal, even in jail. Nevertheless, after reading the summary provided by Alexander the Great, Judge Pereidas looked up and declared, to no one's surprise, "The Court finds probable cause for the charge of murder in the first degree. Are the parties prepared to argue conditions of release?"

That was the part that mattered. At least in the short term, for Hawkins and his family.

"The State is ready, Your Honor," Alexander answered.

Raine confirmed he was ready as well.

"I will hear first from the State," Judge Pereidas said. That was the standard procedure.

"Thank you, Your Honor. The State would ask the Court to set bail at one million dollars," Alexander said. That was the standard bail. "The Court is well aware, as we all are, of the defendant's status within our judicial system. The Court may be tempted to take that status into account, to either the benefit or the detriment of the defendant. I would urge the Court to do neither. Judge Hawkins stands accused of murder in the first degree, and on not insubstantial evidence, I might add. It would be inappropriate to treat him any differently from any other defendant so situated. Indeed, to do so would undercut the faith of all participants in the system, from prosecutors to defense attorneys, defendants to witnesses, members of the bench to members of the public."

It was the argument Raine anticipated. Which was good, because he was ready to respond to it.

"The court rules give clear guidance," Alexander continued, "on what factors should be considered when setting a bail amount. Chief among those considerations are whether the defendant presents a flight risk and whether he presents a danger to others. These are subjective, of course, and ultimately come down to little more than an educated guess by the Court. But here, the Court should be mindful of all the defendant has to lose in the event of a conviction. The minimum sentence is twenty-five years, with a very realistic possibility of more. Given his age, that amounts to a functional life sentence for the defendant. The Canadian border is a short three-hour drive from this courthouse, and a man with the defendant's means, status, education, and experience would be able to wage quite a legal battle to prevent his extradition back to the United States. If he were to choose to flee the jurisdiction, it could be unusually difficult to secure his return."

"I thought he wanted to treat me the same as everyone else," Hawkins complained to Raine under his breath.

"The legal standard is the same," Raine whispered back, "but the facts are unique to each defendant. There's not much that can be more unique than a judge charged with murder."

"As for risk of re-offense," Alexander continued, "I would simply point out that no one would ever have expected a sitting judge of this Superior Court to commit murder even once. How can the Court confidently conclude he might not do it again?"

That seemed like burden shifting to Raine, but he would get his chance to speak, and soon.

"Therefore, Your Honor," Alexander summarized, "for all of the reasons I have just articulated, the State respectfully requests this honorable Court to set bail at the very standard, very justified amount of one million dollars." Then, almost as an afterthought, he added those other conditions of release a judge usually ordered. "We would also ask for no criminal law violations, no contact with the victim's family, remain in contact with defense counsel, and attend all future court dates. Thank you."

"Thank you, Mr. Alexander." Judge Pereidas nodded down to the prosecutor. She then turned to the defense. "Mr. Raine? Would you like to be heard today, or reserve argument?"

A defense attorney had the option to reserve argument, accept the bail amount recommended by the prosecutor, and hope to convince a future judge at a future hearing to reduce that already calcifying bail ruling. There were rare instances where that might be a good idea. Right then was not such an instance.

"Yes, I would like to be heard now, Your Honor," Raine answered.

"Very well." Pereidas nodded. "Please proceed."

"Thank you, Your Honor." Raine took a moment, then launched into his argument. "Equal protection under the law does not mean identical application of the law regardless of individual circumstances. Justice is the result of the interplay between law and facts. The law is the same, case after case after case. The facts are different, case after case after case. Here, I can agree with Mr. Alexander that the Court's primary considerations are whether Judge Hawkins presents a risk to flee or a risk to commit offenses like the one he now finds himself charged with. But I do not agree that the inquiry ends there, although even if it did, the Court should release Judge Hawkins on his own recognizance."

It was a high-level, intellectual introduction. Those were

usually best followed by a low-level engagement of the facts on the ground.

"Judge Hawkins is not a flight risk. He has worked his entire professional life to achieve his current status, a member of the same bench as Your Honor. The only way he retains that achievement is to stand and fight and win, which he has every intention of doing. Similarly, he presents no risk to commit a crime like the one he is charged with. He didn't even commit that crime. To refer to it as 'reoffending' truly puts the cart before the verdict, turning the presumption of innocence on its head. He can't reoffend if he never offended in the first place, which is the situation here."

Raine took a beat to try to assess the impact of his argument on Pereidas, but she maintained a judicially inscrutable expression. She was a good judge. So was Hawkins. Reminding her of that was how he could win the argument.

"But the Court can and must do more than consider those two factors. The Court can and must consider the individualized situation of the defendant. A million dollars is the usual bail on a murder charge. The short drive to Canada is the usual reason the prosecution gives for that recommendation. Fear of additional crimes is the usual reason the Court adopts the recommendation. But this is not the usual case. This is a very unusual case. A singularly unusual case, in fact, as evidenced by the row of news cameras at the back of the gallery."

Raine gestured toward the gallery, and Pereidas and Alexander both glanced again at the collection of reporters and camera operators standing against the far wall.

"Michael Hawkins is a judge," Raine continued. "And not just any judge, but a judge of this very court. A judge who has himself sent countless criminal defendants to the very jail the prosecutor now asks Your Honor to confine him in. That fact, that indisputable, immutable fact must also be taken into consideration when applying the law. The truth of the matter is that Judge Hawkins's physical safety, and indeed his very life, would be at risk in the jail in a way that is simply not the case for any other defendant currently facing charges in this court. To ignore that is to ignore a fact relevant to the Court's determination, and to ignore facts makes justice impossible."

Raine took a moment to look at his client. Hawkins's expression suggested he hadn't considered his actual life might be in danger, but was considering it then.

"The law is filled with exceptions to account for the particularized circumstances of individual defendants," Raine went on. "For example, there are mandatory minimum jail sentences for DUI offenders, but those mandatory sentences can be lessened or even waived altogether if the defendant has a medical condition which would make incarceration dangerous to their health or safety. Judge Hawkins does not have a medical condition that would make holding him on a high bail dangerous to his health or safety, but he does have an occupational condition which does so. Therefore, the Court has an obligation to craft conditions of release which balance the exceedingly miniscule risks of flight or alleged re-offense against the almost certain risk of physical violence against Judge Hawkins if he is needlessly held in custody pending trial."

That was the why. It was finally time for the what.

"Accordingly, the defense respectfully recommends that the Court release Judge Hawkins on his own personal recognizance."

Then it was time for a realistic what. There was no way the judge was going to P.R. a murder defendant without the prosecutor's blessing. Even a judge.

"Short of that," Raine offered the judge a compromise, "the defense would recommend bail in a lower amount of one hundred thousand dollars and house arrest with an electronic monitoring device. We would concur with the other conditions proposed by the State. Thank you."

"I don't want to post a hundred grand," Hawkins whispered to Raine.

"Do you want to post a million?" Raine whispered back out of the corner of his mouth. He kept his eyes on the judge to await her decision.

"May I respond, Your Honor?" Alexander asked.

Raine frowned, but that was also usual procedure. Whoever went first also could ask for the last word.

"Yes, Mr. Alexander," Judge Pereidas allowed. "But briefly."

"Thank you, Your Honor." Alexander somehow stood even straighter than he was already standing. "I would simply point out that Mr. Raine's argument conflates judicial and administrative functions. This Court sets conditions of release as may be appropriate under the law and facts of the case. Then, after that decision is made, the jail will take whatever administrative steps are necessary to effectuate the Court's judicial decision, and in such a way as to protect the safety of the defendant, who is already in their charge. Thank you."

"Thank you, Mr. Alexander." The judge nodded approvingly. She was ready to rule.

Raine interrupted anyway. "May I be allowed the briefest reply, Your Honor?"

Pereidas winced. Judges hated it when legal arguments turned into tennis matches. A response by the moving party was standard. A reply by the respondent was annoying and a gateway to endless back and forth.

"One sentence, Your Honor," Raine implored. "Please."

The judge thought for a moment, then sighed. "One sentence, Mr. Raine."

"Mr. Alexander's response," Raine pointed out, "admits the truth of my argument that holding Judge Hawkins in jail puts his personal safety in jeopardy."

Alexander raised a finger. "May I respond to that?"

"No." Pereidas wagged a finger at both of the lawyers. "I have heard enough. I am ready to rule."

Raine crossed his fingers in his mind. Hawkins exhaled deeply and awaited his fate. Or at least this first part of his fate.

"Both sides make solid arguments," the judge began, "based on reasonable positions, and supported by the law of these hearings and the facts of this case. These arguments and the nature of the case lead me to two separate but unavoidably connected conclusions."

Two? Raine wondered what that meant.

"First, as to bail," Pereidas continued, "I am persuaded to find an accommodation somewhere between the extremes recommended by each advocate. Mr. Raine, I will not release an accused murderer on his personal recognizance, because to do so would ignore the seriousness of the law alleged to have been broken in this case. But Mr. Alexander, I will not set bail at the usual one million dollars, because to do so would ignore the particular facts of this case. I believe the appropriate bail amount lies somewhere between these two positions. Accordingly, I will set bail at five hundred thousand dollars and require the defendant to be on electronic home monitoring should he post that bail. The other conditions suggested by the parties—no criminal law violations, no contact with the family of the alleged victim, and attend all future court dates—will also be imposed."

Pereidas raised her gavel, but held it aloft as she announced her second ruling. "Second, while it was necessary to conduct this hearing today, given the fact that the incident in question occurred just last night, this will be the last hearing presided over by a judge from the King County Superior Court. It will be too difficult to separate the professional relationships the judges of this county have with the defendant, and it will be impossible to avoid the appearance of potential bias, regardless of whether any such bias actually creeps into the proceedings to come. Accordingly, all future hearings will be scheduled in front of a visiting judge to be recruited from another county."

The judge banged her gavel to punctuate her rulings, and the hearing was concluded.

The guards immediately grabbed Hawkins and removed him to the holding cells so the next case could be called. Raine would have time to speak with him in the holding cells before he was returned to the jail. Plenty of time, in fact. All of the inmates for the afternoon calendar had been brought over together, and they would all return together. Hawkins would sit in a cell until the last of them had been seen by the judge.

"Nice argument," Raine remarked to Alexander as they stepped away from the bar. "I'm not sure who won."

"I believe we both lost," Alexander answered. "A draw. At least in the courtroom. The true winner will be evident once it's determined whether your client can post the half-million bail."

Raine nodded. "Agreed. I guess I'll go talk to him about that."

"Excellent," Alexander replied, turning toward the exit. "I will see you next at the pretrial conference. Don't expect me to offer any reduction in charges."

"And don't expect me to plead my client guilty to something he didn't do," Raine called after him.

It was going to be a trial.

"HALF A MILLION DOLLARS?" Hawkins shook his head as he and Raine reconnected inside an attorney-client meeting booth connected to the holding cells. "I don't have half a million dollars."

"What about your house?" Raine suggested. "How much equity do you have in it?"

"Nowhere near that much." Hawkins shook his head. "We've taken out a bunch of home equity loans, first to pay my campaign and then to pay for Trevor's college. There's nothing left to pull out of it. Not a half mil anyway."

"Maybe if you sold it?" Raine wondered. "It seems like home prices in Seattle go up by the minute."

"No, that's not fair to Cindy and Trevor." Hawkins shook his head again. "Plus, it would take too long. I need to get out of here as soon as possible. You weren't wrong about me being in danger in here."

"Well," Raine rubbed his chin, "we both know you don't need the full five-hundred-thousand. You need only ten percent of that, fifty thousand, and collateral. Then you can get a bonding company to post it."

"Maybe," Hawkins allowed begrudgingly. "If they accept a completely mortgaged house as collateral, and they're willing to take the risk that I don't drive to Canada like you mentioned."

"You won't flee to Canada," Raine answered. "If you did that, the bonding company would take the house, and your family would be out on the street. You may not be a murderer, but you're a good husband and father. I can vouch for that."

"Vouch to whom?" Hawkins questioned.

Raine grinned. "I know a guy."

8

The guy in question was named Sebastian Yu. He was the owner and operator of Screaming Eagle Bail Bonds, located conveniently across Third Avenue from the King County Courthouse. Fancy civil attorneys in large corporate firms developed relationships with financial advisors and fund managers. Solo practitioners who needed to take criminal cases to keep the lights on developed relationships with substance abuse treatment providers and bail bondsmen. Raine had sent enough business Yu's way that Yu owed him a favor. At least, Raine hoped as much when he pulled open the business's iron-barred door and stepped inside.

The interior was dim, almost dank. The only windows were on either side of the front door, and in addition to sporting their own sets of iron bars, they had been painted over to block the view of the intractable homeless encampment outside. The city had long ago decided to let it fester there rather than disperse it and allow it to reform somewhere the tourists might see it. That stretch of sidewalk had been covered in a rotating cast of homeless people and their tents for as long as Raine had been an attorney.

That was getting to be a long time, Raine was reminded, as he spied the only employee inside: a young woman half his age, probably younger. She wore a sleeveless silk blouse with an open collar that showed off the tapestry of tattoos on her throat and arms. The one on her left shoulder wasn't complete yet, but the initial line work was strong. She had short black hair and heavy makeup that looked like it had been applied by a professional cosmetics artist. Her fingers and wrists were covered in jewelry that clacked as she typed at her computer. She looked up at Raine as he entered, but didn't greet him because she was on the phone, speaking into a headset in a language that was definitely not English. She raised a manicured, blood-red fingernail at him, and he tried to guess what language she was speaking as she concluded the conversation.

"Thank you for waiting," she said to Raine after ending the call. She pushed the microphone of her headset away from her mouth, her lipstick the same shade as her nails. "May I help you, sir?"

"Was that Italian?" Raine asked. "It wasn't Spanish." Raine couldn't speak Spanish, but he could recognize it.

"Portuguese," the woman answered. "Many of our clients speak a first language other than English. May I help you?" she repeated.

"Is Mr. Yu available?" Raine asked.

"Do you have an appointment?" the woman asked, glancing at her computer monitor, where Sebastian Yu's calendar would clearly show that Raine did not have an appointment.

"No, but I think he'll see me," Raine replied. "I refer a lot of business here, and I have a client who needs a little extra attention."

"You're an attorney." It was more a statement than a question. Raine was still in his suit.

"Guilty," Raine joked. "Dan Raine, attorney at law, at your service."

The woman nodded but didn't offer her name in return. Instead, she pulled the headset microphone back in front of her mouth, looked again to her computer screen, and clicked her computer mouse a few times.

"There's a Mr. Raine in the lobby, sir," she said after a moment. "He doesn't have an appointment."

"You left out the lawyer part," Raine half-whispered to her.

She looked at him, large green eyes outlined in thick black eyeliner, but didn't add the information. Instead, she nodded several times at whatever her boss was saying, then ended the call. She looked again to Raine, only long enough to say, "Mr. Yu will be out shortly."

Raine felt an urge to engage her in further small talk while he waited to see her boss, but she immediately began another phone call, again in a language Raine didn't know, but a new one. Mandarin, perhaps? Whatever it was, she was fluent in it.

Raine took a seat in a stuffed green leather chair near the windows. The silhouette of a small tent was discernible despite the paint. Raine checked the time. The courthouse would be open for another couple of hours. Hawkins could be out of jail that night if Raine could convince Yu he owed him a favor that big.

"Dan!" Yu came gliding out of his office, which was mostly hidden in the far corner of the otherwise open space.

"To what do I owe the pleasure of this in-person visit? Usually, you just send the client or his family here with one of your business cards."

Yu was a tall man and a sharp dresser. He wore the vest and pants of a gray three-piece suit; the jacket was likely on a hanger on the back of his office door. A crisp white shirt covered his arms, and a striped blue tie adorned his neck. His shoes were polished to a mirror-like shine. Bail bonds could be a lucrative business.

"A friend is in trouble," Raine explained. "Can we talk in your office?"

"Of course," Yu agreed. He gestured at the young woman Raine had just been speaking to. "But Edna will know everything as soon as we're done. She's the one who will process the paperwork for your friend."

Raine glanced again at the young woman. He didn't think she looked very much like an 'Edna'. But he liked that Yu was already expecting to post the bond for Raine's friend.

"By the way, how many languages does Edna speak?" he asked in a lowered voice.

Yu smiled and shrugged. "I'm not done counting yet."

"Your friend is Judge Hawkins?" Yu slapped his forehead after Raine identified his client and the trouble he was in. "And he's charged with murder? Oh, Dan. I can see why you came in person. What's the bail? A million? Two?"

"I got it down to a half mil," Raine answered, "but he doesn't have that kind of money. Not liquid anyway. He needs a bond."

"Sure, sure." Yu opened a desk drawer and pulled out

some standard forms and a pen. "It's usually ten percent fee, but for you, I'll lower it to forty-five thousand. I'll need a cashier's check or a wire transfer. We'll need to hurry if you want me to post it before the court closes today."

Raine took a deep breath. "Well, there's a small catch."

Yu looked at Raine for a moment, then set down the pen and leaned back in his chair. "What's the catch?"

"He doesn't really have fifty thousand liquid either," Raine answered.

"Forty-five," Yu corrected.

"Or forty-five," Raine amended. "He's going to need a payment plan. And nothing down."

"Nothing down?" Yu barked out a laugh. "Nothing down and I post a half mil? Does he want a ride home from the jail too? Maybe I can bake him some cookies for the trip?"

"He's good for it, Sebastian," Raine insisted. "He's a judge, for God's sake. He's not going anywhere. You'll get your money back from the court at the end of the case."

"Canada is a very short drive from here." Yu pointed vaguely north.

"I'm aware," Raine acknowledged, "but he's not going to flee to Canada. He has a wife and a kid and a job, all here. Also, he's innocent."

Yu laughed again. "I don't care if he's innocent. If I only did business with innocent clients, I wouldn't be in business very long. And neither would you."

Raine nodded. "Yeah, I know. It doesn't matter to you. But it matters to me."

"It shouldn't," Yu castigated. "You have a job to do, whether he's guilty or innocent. But so do I. I can't post half a million dollars on nothing but a signature on a promissory note."

"You can," Raine corrected.

Yu frowned. "I shouldn't."

Raine noted he didn't say, 'I won't.'

"What do you need to get this done, Sebastian?" Raine asked. "Name it and I'll make it happen."

"You pay the forty-five thousand," Yu answered.

"Me, personally?" Raine shook his head. "I can't do that. It's against the ethical rules. I'd lose my license. You know that."

"I do know that. I also know people break the rules sometimes for friends." He sighed, then nodded toward the lobby and the exit beyond. "Can you do anything about that homeless camp on my front doorstep? The city won't do anything. They're just glad they're here by the courthouse and not down at the waterfront. But it's bad for business, even my business. My clients don't care that much, but my employees do. I can't keep any staff. Edna just started, and she's already the best assistant I've ever had. I don't want to lose her too. I need those people gone."

Raine turned to look out toward the lobby as well. "You want me to clear out a block-long homeless encampment? Like, just start pushing people away? That would never work. There are way too many of them. And the cops would arrest me for assault if I tried."

"Maybe your judge friend can issue an order to make them leave," Yu suggested.

"In exchange for special consideration on his bond agreement?" Raine questioned. "That sounds like a bribe."

Yu threw Raine a sideways grin. "Oh, is that now a problem for Judge Hawkins?"

Raine narrowed his eyes. "What are you suggesting?"

Another shrug. "I hear things. People say things. I just

mean, maybe your friend isn't as trustworthy as you think. If he misses even one court date, I lose five hundred thousand dollars. And I can't send a bounty hunter into Canada to get him back."

Raine closed his eyes and rubbed the bridge of his nose. "I think I might be able to help you find better office space. Still close to the courthouse, same rent, but without the tent city on the front sidewalk." He looked up at Yu again. "If I promise to do that, will you agree to post the bond?"

Yu crossed his arms. "How are you going to do that?"

Raine sighed. "I know a gal."

9

R ebecca Sommers. Executive Realtor. The number one commercial real estate agent in Seattle, Downtown core and First Hill regions. Part-time investigator. Everyone had a side hustle nowadays.

"Is Ms. Sommers expecting you?" asked the receptionist when Raine showed up unannounced. He'd come directly from the bail bonds company. Time was running out to get Hawkins's bail posted before the court closed for the day.

"No," Raine admitted. It was a day of meetings without appointments. "Tell her it's Dan Raine and I need her help."

The receptionist frowned at him. She was a young woman with black hair and brown eyes. She looked like she enjoyed her job and didn't want to risk it on some random man she didn't know.

"I'm a lawyer," Raine expanded. "We work together sometimes."

"On deals?" the woman inquired.

"Sure," Raine answered. *Plea deals, maybe*, he thought. "I

really do need to talk with her, and now. Time is of the essence."

That was one of those legal phrases that had made it into the common vernacular. The receptionist didn't understand the significance of the phrase in a legal context, but she knew it meant whatever Raine needed to talk to her boss about, it was time-sensitive.

"I'll see if she's available," the woman finally agreed. Her fingers danced across her keyboard, and after a minute or so, she looked up again. "Ms. Sommers is available. She says you can go back to her office. Do you know where it is?"

Raine nodded. "Yes. I've been here before. Thanks for your help."

He walked the corridor to Sommers's office and stopped in the doorway, knocking twice on the doorframe. Sommers looked up from her computer. She was dressed to impress in a navy blue business suit and pearls, her long platinum hair cascading over one shoulder. Raine always felt underdressed when he was with her, even when he was wearing a suit like then.

"Dan," she greeted him with a broad smile. "To what do I owe this unexpected, and unscheduled, visit?"

"Haven't you heard the news?" Raine asked. "I thought you might be expecting me."

"No." Sommers shook her head. "I just got back from Aspen."

"Aspen?" Raine scoffed as he stepped into the office. "Do people really go there?"

Sommers crossed her arms. "I do."

"My last vacation was car camping with my boys at Hood Canal," Raine replied.

"You know that's not really a vacation, right?" Sommers returned.

Raine shrugged. "My boys liked it."

"I'm sure that's what matters," Sommers offered. "But back to this news. I assume it's local to Seattle if I didn't hear about it in Colorado?"

"Very local," Raine confirmed. "King County. More specifically, the King County Superior Court."

"That's really more your territory," Sommers said. "What's going on? And why do I need to know about it?"

"Do you remember my old law partner?" Raine asked. "It was his name they were scraping off the front window when you tried to sell my office out from under me."

Sommers shook a finger at her guest. "I was just doing my job. It's not my fault you were going to struggle to make rent without your partner. But it all worked out in the end."

That was true, Raine supposed.

"So, what about him?" Sommers asked. "He became a judge or something, right? Did something happen to him?"

"You might say that," Raine answered. "Or it's going to, if I don't stop it."

Then Raine explained what had happened. Trevor, Szabo, the blackmail, the fundraiser, the gunshot, Lydia, the arrest, the charges, and the arraignment. He paused before reaching the part about the bail.

"That's terrible," Sommers replied. "So, you need an investigator again? Someone you can trust? You got it, Dan. It's the least I can do after trying to flip your office. What are we doing first? Interviewing witnesses? Tailing suspects? A little breaking and entering after dark? That's always fun."

"Maybe all of that, eventually," Raine answered, "but

there's a little something first. A little favor." It was his day to call in favors.

Sommers may have been his increasingly regular private investigator, but she was a businessperson first. "Favor?" she questioned with narrowed eyes. "What kind of favor?"

So, Raine explained the rest. The bail amount. Sebastian Yu. The homeless encampment on Third Avenue. Even Edna, for some reason.

"You committed me to a business relationship without checking with me?" Sommers frowned at Raine.

"You don't think you can do it?" Raine responded.

Sommers's frown faded. "Don't change the subject."

"I'm not," Raine replied. "I wouldn't have suggested it if I didn't think you could do it. And if you can't, then all that means is I was wrong. Oh, and my friend probably gets shanked in the shower and dies."

Sommers crossed her arms again and stared at Raine for several seconds. "Really?"

"Maybe," Raine answered. "They'll try to protect him. Maybe. A little. But if someone wants to hurt him, they will."

Sommers uncrossed her arms and drummed her fingers on the desk. "I'm not splitting the commission with you. No referral fee or anything like that."

"Of course not," Raine agreed. "I wouldn't think of it."

Sommers picked up the phone. "What's the guy's name again?"

"Sebastian Yu."

"Ruby," Sommers said into the phone, "get me Sebastian Yu on the line." Then, to Raine, "What's the name of his business?"

"Screaming Eagle Bail Bonds."

Sommers took a beat. "Seriously?"

"It's marketing." Raine shrugged. "There's nothing quite so American as breaking the law."

Sommers sighed, then passed the information to her assistant, "Sebastian Yu. Screaming Eagle Bail Bonds. Tell him I'm a friend of Dan Raine and I hear he's looking for some new office space. Call me back when you have him on the line."

She hung up the phone, and Raine thanked her.

"Whatever." Sommers waved the thanks away. "Now, what's the play? Did your friend do it? I guess that's not supposed to matter, right?"

"It's not," Raine answered, "and he didn't. At least he says he didn't."

"And you believe him?"

"I'm choosing to believe him," Raine admitted.

Sommers nodded several times. "Okay, okay. And I learned from you that if our client didn't do it, then someone else did. So who are we going to pin this on? Who are our other suspects?"

Raine appreciated that Sommers had been listening to him over their partnership. "There are two possibilities, but one of them is kind of a nonstarter."

"What do you mean?" Sommers questioned. "Why?"

"Because the best suspect is Hawkins's son, Trevor," Raine answered. "He had an argument with her that night and knew where the gun was. Motive, means, and as much opportunity as anyone other than Hawkins himself. But Hawkins would never let us blame the murder on his own son. He'd plead guilty before he let that happen."

Sommers raised a fist to her lips and nodded. "I guess I can respect that. So, who's the other suspect?"

"Emil Szabo," Raine answered. "Lydia's father and the head of a rich and ruthless crime family."

"Her father?" Sommers questioned. "Your friend won't let his child go to prison, but you think this guy would murder his kid?"

"They're very different people," Raine answered. "Hawkins hired me to help his son. Szabo carved his son's eye out. I have no doubt he would kill her if he felt she had betrayed him, or to prevent her from doing so."

Sommers relaxed her fist and tapped her lips. "Was he there that night? I can't believe he was on the guest list."

"He was definitely not on the guest list," Raine agreed. "And I didn't see him. But maybe somebody else did. Someone who was part of the background and Szabo wouldn't have been as careful about avoiding."

"The hired help," Sommers said.

"Exactly."

"The butler saw it," Sommers added with a chuckle.

"Something like that," Raine agreed. "So, that's where we start. Talking to—"

The ring of Sommers's phone interrupted his proposal.

Sommers held a finger up to him and answered the phone. "Ruby? Yes. Put him on." Then a whisper to Raine. "It's your bail bond guy."

Raine allowed a smile. At least something was going right, finally.

"Mr. Yu!" Sommers enthused into the phone. "I believe you and I have a connection in common. Attorney Dan Raine. He's sitting in my office right now, and he tells me you might be in need of my services... Yes. Exactly... Oh, I have several properties in mind already... Of course, of course. Let's schedule a meeting. But first, I believe there's the small matter of a bond to post and only an hour or so before the court closes."

Raine gave Sommers a thumbs-up. She returned the gesture.

"Yes, well, I'm afraid that matter is a precondition of my services," Sommers continued. "Take care of that, then call my office and schedule a time with Ruby. You will be in a far better location in no time at all."

Sommers reaffirmed her commitment to help Yu and the necessity of him helping Raine, then terminated the call to give Yu enough time to get the bond posted.

She hung up and smiled broadly at Raine. "Task one accomplished," she said. "Now, let's figure out who we're going to talk to first. I assume there was no actual butler?"

"There was no butler," Raine confirmed. "But there were valets."

10

It was a simple matter to get the names of the valet and catering vendors from Cindy. It was a bit more complicated to determine exactly which employees were there that night. And to decide in what order to interview them.

"Let's start from the outside in," was Raine's suggestion when he and Sommers reassembled the next morning at Raine's office to begin their investigation in earnest. "In the order an uninvited guest would be seen. First, the valet, then the caterer. We talk to those off-duty cops last."

"Why?" Sommers questioned. "Isn't it possible they saw someone first? They were supposed to be patrolling the perimeter, right?"

"Well, yes," Raine allowed, "but they'll just support the official police conclusion that Hawkins was the shooter, unless we can give them a reason to open up to us. Hopefully, we get that from either the valets or the caterers."

The office for Silver Star Valet Services was located in the light industrial area south of downtown, in a single-story strip mall of offices for businesses that didn't need a sales floor for potential customers. Its immediate neighbors were a trophy store and a tool rental business. A steady afternoon rain had settled in, pulling the scent of dirt and gasoline from the asphalt. Raine parked directly in front of the valet business. All the spots were empty.

"What's our cover story?" Sommers asked. "We're a pair of tech wiz-kids hosting a party for wealthy donors we want to invest in our latest app?"

Raine blinked at her. "Well, that does sound fun," he allowed, "but I'm not sure how we bring up the whole murder at the Hawkins home thing. Let's just play this straight. I'm his lawyer, you're my investigator, and we want to talk to some potential witnesses to see if they saw anything unusual."

Sommers frowned. "Can I at least be a whiz-kid investigator?"

Raine gave her a wink as he opened his door. "You already are."

They walked quickly through the rain to the front door of Silver Star Valet. Raine held the door for Sommers, then ducked in after her. Inside, there was little more than a counter with no one behind it and some framed testimonials on the wall above a row of three uncomfortable-looking chairs. Their entrance had set off an electronic bell, and after a few moments, a large man emerged through the door to the back of the business.

"Hello. Welcome to Silver Star Valet Services, Seattle's premier event valet provider," he greeted them in a gravelly voice. He had black hair and a dark five o'clock shadow several hours early. "How can I make your event a success?"

Raine appreciated the marketing integrated into the

welcome. "Actually, we were hoping to talk to a few people about a past event that wasn't very successful."

The man's practiced expression dropped. "I'm sorry to hear that, sir. Are you here to submit a complaint about one of our Silver Star team members?"

"Oh, no, nothing like that," Raine assured with a slight wave of his hand. "Your Silver Star team members did an excellent job, I'm sure. It's just that the evening ended poorly for other reasons."

The man cocked his head slightly.

"Someone was murdered," Sommers put in. "We'd like to talk to the valets who were working that night to see if they saw anything."

The man nodded. "Oh yes. I heard about that. Two of our valets were detained for questioning. We had to pay them overtime."

Raine smiled slightly at the payroll issue being the main concern of their host. "Could we get some contact information for those two valets? We'd like to ask them a few questions."

"Are you the police?" the man asked.

"No," Raine answered. "We represent the man accused of the murder."

"Falsely accused," Sommers added. "That's important."

It was, Raine agreed silently, but only if the man believed them. He wondered whether he would.

The man crossed his arms and thought for several moments. "You don't really know that for certain, do you?"

Sommers looked to Raine to respond.

"Not any more than the police know he's guilty," Raine answered. "That's why we're here. That's why we need to speak to your Silver Star team members."

The man stared at Raine for several seconds, then uncrossed his arms and reached for the pen and pad next to the sole computer on the counter. "Marcus and Simone. They were the ones who put in for overtime. We paid it, of course. The police wouldn't let them leave. This is different. If they agree to talk to you, they do it on their own time. Let them know that."

He slid over a piece of paper with the employees' names and phone numbers.

Raine picked up the note and held it up to the man. "We'll tell them. Thank you."

The man nodded. "I hope the truth comes out. Whatever that may be."

"We hope so, too," Sommers responded.

MARCUS ANSWERED his phone on the first try, so he was the one they spoke to first. As they might have guessed, he didn't support himself solely from valet gigs on weekends. That was a side hustle, one of many. His main job was waiting tables at a fancy seafood restaurant on the waterfront. He also had an online shop of homemade jewelry.

"You can't make ends meet with just one job anymore," Marcus explained. He gestured at the clientele of the restaurant, less than half full in the lull between lunch and dinner. "Not unless you're a tech bro or you inherited money. Someone like me? I'm always hustling."

He was young, early twenties at most, with thin features and short bleached hair. His nose and lip were pierced, and his earlobes housed quarter-sized gauges. There were no tattoos visible, but Raine guessed that was only due to the long sleeves on his work shirt.

"I understand," Sommers answered. "This is my side hustle too."

Marcus narrowed his eyes at them. "Who do you represent again?"

"We represent Judge Michael Hawkins," Raine answered. "He was the one who hosted the party. He's the one the police arrested for murder."

"He killed someone at his own party?" Marcus shook his head. "That's just stupid. It's like inviting a hundred witnesses."

"It would be stupid," Raine agreed, "if he'd done it. But he didn't. That's why we're here."

"If he didn't do it, why did he get arrested?" Marcus challenged.

"You ever been accused of something you didn't do?" Raine asked.

"Or maybe something you did do," Sommers suggested, "but no one could prove?"

Marcus pointed at Sommers. "That second one, maybe. Okay, fine. What do you want from me? I was outside when the gunshot went off. I didn't see anything."

"No one saw what happened when the gun went off," Raine asserted. "We want to know what you saw before and after that."

"Like what?" Marcus shrugged. "Beforehand, it was just a bunch of old people with money handing me their keys and a tip. Afterward, it was just craziness. Everybody either running inside or running away."

"Did anybody try to get their car out immediately after the gunshot?" Sommers asked.

"A bunch of people did," Marcus answered. "It was scary. People wanted to leave."

"Did any of them seem more than scared?" Raine asked. "More like nervous?"

"Nervous?" Marcus asked.

"Anxious?" Raine tried.

"Anxious?"

"Oh, for God's sake." Sommers threw her hands up. "Did any of them look like they just shot somebody and were trying to get away?"

Raine appreciated Sommers's bluntness, but he didn't expect that question to garner a helpful answer. He was wrong.

"Well..." Marcus rubbed his chin. "There was this one guy. An older guy, like late fifties, maybe early sixties? Gray hair, beard, nice suit. He was the only one who was calm. He walked right up to Simone and gave her a hundred to get his car first."

"Did she?"

"For a hundred bucks?" Marcus laughed. "Hell, yes."

"Did you notice anything else about him?" Raine asked. There was one detail he really wanted to hear.

Marcus twisted his mouth up as he recalled the event. "I think he had an accent. Not like a really obvious one, but it was still there. Almost like an actor, you know?"

"I do know," Raine answered.

Raine thanked Marcus, and they let him get back to work before the dinner rush started.

"Did that description match Emil Szabo?" Sommers asked on their way back to Raine's car.

Raine nodded. "Perfectly."

SIMONE CAVANAUGH WAS a student at Seattle University, up the hill and east of downtown. The campus filled the space between the medical buildings of First Hill to the south and the gay bars of Capitol Hill to the north. Working as a valet on the weekends was how she got spending money while she worked toward her nursing degree—including an extra hundred dollars for helping a murderer escape, maybe. Raine wasn't about to frame it like that. Not right then to her. But maybe later to the jury.

"Thanks for agreeing to meet with us," Raine began their conversation. They were inside the student union building. It wasn't the most private location, but the rain hadn't let up, so they couldn't sit outside. They would have to settle for the anonymity of a disinterested crowd.

"Do you remember an older man with gray hair and a beard?" Raine jumped right in after the introductions and entreaty to help them. "He gave you a hundred-dollar tip."

"Oh, I remember him," Simone answered. She was petite, with brown curls down her back and freckles behind large, round glasses. "And he tipped me a hundred and fifty."

"A hundred and fifty?" Raine questioned.

"To get his car out first?" Sommers followed up.

"Sort of," Simone answered. "Fifty when he got there, for me to park it in the driveway instead of three blocks up the street like everybody else. Then another hundred to jump to the front of the line when people started panicking after the gunshot."

"Did you do both of those things?" Raine asked.

"Damn right I did." Simone laughed. "I'm a college student at a private school on the West Coast. It's stupidly expensive here. A hundred and fifty bucks might not be much to a fancy lawyer and his even fancier investigator— I love your dress, by the way—but it's a lot of money to me."

Raine wasn't going to begrudge the woman an overly generous tip. In fact, it helped his case. He was about to ask another question when she helped him even more.

"In fact," she went on, "when he handed me the keys and the fifty, he asked me if I ever did any modeling. He said a girl like me could earn a lot on the side with the right connections. I was going to ask him about it when he picked his car up, but he was in too much of a hurry. You don't happen to know his name, do you?"

"Em—" Sommers started to answer, but Raine cut her off.

"No, we don't," he said. "We're trying to find out who he is, too."

Out of the corner of his eye, Raine could see Sommers looking askance at him. He ignored her. "What kind of car was it?" he asked Simone. "Was it nice?"

"Oh yeah, real nice," Simone answered. "Some sort of luxury sedan. Shiny and black. It was pretty lit."

"Okay. Was there anything about the man himself?" Raine asked. "Marcus mentioned a slight accent. Did you notice that? Maybe a unique piece of jewelry? Anything?"

Simone thought for a moment. "I didn't notice any jewelry. And the accent was really faint, like barely at all. Maybe he was Canadian or something?"

"Okay," Raine accepted the information as neutrally as he could. Emil Szabo wasn't Canadian.

"Sorry I can't be more helpful," Simone offered. "I guess I wasn't paying that much attention. Honestly, I was looking at that hundred-dollar bill and wondering if I could make more of those."

"Stay in nursing school," Raine counseled as he stood up. "You don't want to earn money from a man like that."

"I thought you said you didn't know him," Simone questioned.

"I know men like him," Raine answered. "Thank you for your time. You should get back to your studies."

LA FRAISE FRAICHE CATERING was far closer to its downtown corporate clients than Silver Star Valet. Located in the ground floor of the Seattle Municipal Tower at the corner of Sixth and Cherry, it was only a few blocks from the courthouse. It served pastries and espresso during the day in addition to catering private lunches and after-hours events. Raine had enjoyed a beignet or two from them over the years, but he'd never had them cater a party. Then again, he'd never run for judge.

Unlike the valets, the catering staff at *La Fraise Fraiche* were regular employees, not part-time gig workers. And most of them were working that day.

"Oh my God," the woman working the front counter gasped when Raine explained why they had come. "A murder? That's so terrible. So, so terrible. Let me get Linda. She was there that night. She can help you."

Raine thanked the woman and turned around to see a crowd of café patrons staring at them. The woman behind the counter had not been quiet when she shouted 'murder'.

"Hello?" A voice rang out from behind the counter. A tall woman with a hairnet full of blonde curls and a smear of flour on her cheek came out from the kitchen area. "I'm Linda, the day manager. Clarissa said you wanted to talk to someone about the Hawkins event?"

"That's right," Raine confirmed. He recognized her from the front door of the fundraiser.

"And who are you exactly?" Linda asked, crossing her arms. "You look familiar."

"I'm Judge Hawkins's attorney," Raine answered. "And this is my investigator, Rebecca Sommers. Judge Hawkins has been charged with the murder. We're investigating a lead that someone else was the real killer. Someone who wasn't on the guest list."

"Well, I was in charge of the guest list that night," Linda answered. "I can assure you no one came through that front door who wasn't on the list."

"What about the back door?" Sommers asked.

"Good question," Raine affirmed. "I know I saw people coming and going through the back door."

Linda frowned for a moment, then turned and shouted into the back. "Jimmy! Get out here!"

A few moments later, a small and slender young man slipped out from the kitchen. He was no more than 5'6" and looked like he weighed 100 pounds soaking wet. Raine guessed his age to be whatever the absolute youngest age a person could legally work. Fifteen and a half, maybe, if Linda was his mother.

"Yeah, Mom?"

Raine smiled at his own powers of deduction.

"These people want to know if anyone suspicious came in through the back door of the Hawkins house the night of the murder."

Jimmy's eyes widened a bit and his lips pulled into an

anxious grimace. "I'm not sure. There were a lot of people there that night. Like, what kind of person?"

Raine stepped forward and extracted his phone. He had managed to find a single photo of Emil Szabo on the internet, even if it wasn't very good. Blurry and from a distance, but it showed off his basic features. "This person."

Jimmy squinted at Raine's screen and shrugged. "I mean, maybe. He does look kind of familiar. Like, when?"

"Shortly before the murder," Sommers answered.

"Immediately before," Raine added.

Jimmy stared at the photo for several more seconds. "Was he wearing a gray suit?"

Raine nodded eagerly. "Yes. Exactly."

"Yeah, I remember that guy." Jimmy nodded. "I remember him because he looked kind of angry, and I stepped out of his way. He was walking really fast."

"With a purpose," Sommers said to Raine.

Raine nodded to her, then back to Jimmy. "Thank you, son. That's very helpful."

Jimmy frowned a bit at the word 'son', then looked back to his mother. "Can I go back to work now?"

"Absolutely," Linda answered. She watched after him as he disappeared back into the kitchen, then turned back to Raine. "He's not going to have to testify, is he? He's only sixteen."

Raine shrugged. "It depends."

"On what?"

"On whether I can convince the prosecutor that Emil Szabo murdered his own daughter," Raine answered. "If not, then your son will have to help me convince the jury."

11

Sebastian Yu came through for Raine, and Screaming Eagle Bail Bonds posted Hawkins's bail before the court closed.

Raine had given his client a day to spend with his family while he and Sommers interviewed overlooked witnesses. But one day was enough. There was work to do, and Hawkins wasn't a typical client. Not only was he a judge, he was a lawyer. That meant he could help direct the case. For better or worse, Raine knew. But he also knew Hawkins wasn't going to just sit back and let him make all the decisions. They say a defendant who represents themselves has a fool for a lawyer. Representing another lawyer was almost as bad.

"Laura!" Hawkins called out when he arrived at Raine's office first thing the next morning. "It's been too long."

Raine's administrative assistant, and only employee, rushed out from behind her desk to give her old boss a hug. "That's your fault. You never visit."

Hawkins nodded. "That's true. And I'm sorry. It shouldn't take something like this to bring me back to my old office."

"I hate to break up the reunion," Raine said, very much breaking up the reunion, "but I'm eager to give you the update from yesterday. Things are developing in the right direction. We need to discuss next steps."

"Of course, Dan," Hawkins replied. "Good to see you again, Laura."

"You too, Mike," Laura replied before correcting herself. "I mean, Judge Hawkins. Do you still take your coffee the same? Two creams, one sugar?"

"Exactly," Hawkins confirmed. "Great memory."

"For now," Laura answered. "But I'm starting to get too old for this. Mr. Raine has me running more than I did when there were two of you."

"Is that right, Dan?" Hawkins asked. "Business is booming?"

"I wouldn't say that," Raine answered. "Honestly, I almost lost the place when you left. But I had a couple of high-profile cases, and I've clawed my way back a bit."

"High profile, huh?" Hawkins replied. "I bet this one is pretty high profile, too."

"The highest so far," Raine answered. "That's the only reason I took it. You can't buy this type of publicity."

"You better win," Hawkins warned.

Raine smiled and patted him on the shoulder. "That's the plan, friend. Come on. Rebecca is already in the conference room. Laura will bring the coffee in a minute."

Laura confirmed as much and set off for the kitchenette. Raine and Hawkins walked to the conference room. Sommers was typing on her phone when they entered.

"Rebecca Sommers," Raine commenced the introductions, "this is Judge Michael Hawkins. Mike, this is Rebecca Sommers, regularly the number one commercial real estate agent in Seattle and less regularly my investigator. She's also the reason your bail bond was posted."

"I heard," Hawkins replied. "Thank you very much for that, Ms. Sommers."

"Sure," Sommers said without looking up or halting her typing. "Give me a second."

"Working on a big deal?" Hawkins asked.

"Always," Sommers answered. She typed a few more words, tapped 'Send' with a flourish, and finally set her phone down. "This side gig is fun, but it's not going to pay all the bills. Not mine, anyway." She stood up and extended a hand for a proper greeting. "Nice to meet you, Judge Hawkins. It's good to finally put a face to the name."

"The name you had scraped off the window," Raine quipped.

"You did that." Sommers frowned at him. "'And Raine, Attorneys at Law'. Catchy."

Laura brought the coffees in then, before quickly departing and closing the door behind her.

"Alright then," Hawkins started the meeting. "What's the update? When is my case getting dismissed?"

"Not yet," Raine answered with a light laugh.

"But we're working on it," Sommers added.

"We interviewed some witnesses yesterday," Raine expounded. "Two of the valets and a couple people from the caterer. They saw someone who matched Lydia's father's description."

Hawkins's jaw tightened. "Emil Szabo was in my home?"

"Ordinarily, I would say that would be worth getting

upset about," Raine acknowledged his friend's reaction, "but in this case, it's a good thing."

"He arrived shortly before the murder," Sommers said, "and left immediately after. And in a hurry, at that."

"How didn't I see him?" Hawkins wondered.

"You were probably in your bedroom, smoking," Raine answered. "He must have found Lydia and confronted her."

"In my study?" Hawkins questioned. "Why would she have been in my study?"

"Snooping around for something more to blackmail you with?" Raine suggested. "Or maybe Szabo took her upstairs to confront her where no one would see them."

"Does it matter?" Sommers asked.

"It might," Raine answered. "The jury will want to know as many details as possible. That's how they'll decide if it's believable."

"The jury." Hawkins shook his head. "I still can't believe I'm charged with murder. This is crazy."

"Yes, it is," Raine agreed. "There's a chance we can get Alexander to dismiss it, if we can convince him it was Szabo."

"That seems unlikely," Hawkins admitted. "Unless you can get him to confess."

"He doesn't seem like the type of man who would confess to his crimes," Raine replied. "Hard to run a crime syndicate if you confess to everything."

"If you can't convince the prosecutor," Sommers asked, "how will you convince the jury?"

"We don't have to," Hawkins answered. "Not entirely, anyway."

"We just have to make them think it's a reasonable possibility," Raine explained. "Reasonable possibility equals reasonable doubt. And reasonable doubt equals not guilty."

"Did you talk to the cops, too?" Hawkins asked. "They're the ones who will have the most sway with the jury. Not a valet or a caterer."

Raine shook his head. "No, not yet. I want more before I confront them. They aren't going to go against the official line unless they have to. I prefer to question cops on the stand, under oath."

Hawkins frowned slightly. "Yeah, but I know those guys. I hired them specifically because I got to know them over the years. They're solid. They won't lie."

"Maybe, maybe not." Raine wasn't convinced.

"What more do you need?" Hawkins questioned. "You just said you have multiple witnesses who saw Szabo enter the house."

"I said multiple witnesses saw someone who matched Szabo's description," Raine corrected. "Only one of them saw him go inside, and that witness is sixteen years old. I'd like more."

"So, get it from the cops," Hawkins repeated. "I agree that Alexander won't care what a sixteen-year-old kid says, but he will definitely care what a sixteen-year veteran cop says."

Raine ran a hand over his head. "I'm not sure now is the best time to do it. The pretrial is coming up. Maybe we wait to see what Alexander says. Give him a chance to tell us exactly what he needs to dump the case. Then we go out and get that for him."

"Or show up at the pretrial with that information already in hand," Hawkins countered. "If one of these cops can identify Szabo from that night, maybe Alexander agrees to dismiss pending further investigation."

"Or tip off the cops to what we're trying to do," Raine returned, "and give them and Alexander time to shore up their case and discredit our theory."

"Did you guys argue like this when you were still partners?" Sommers asked. "How did you ever get anything done?"

"We had separate cases," Raine explained.

"Separate roles," Hawkins added. "Like now. I'm the client. I get the final say on what we do."

Raine grinned but shook his head. "No, the client gets final say on decisions that involve waiving constitutional rights, like whether to testify, or pleading guilty. The lawyer makes the decisions about strategy."

"It's not quite that simple," Hawkins replied, "but it doesn't matter. This is my case. My life. My family. I don't really care whether you listen to me as your client. Listen to me as your friend. Those cops will help us."

Raine pushed himself back in his chair and sighed. "I'll listen to you," he said, "but I'm telling you, you're wrong. Cops don't help defendants unless they're forced to. I can only force them when I have them on the stand."

"I have confidence in you," Hawkins assured him.

Raine decided not to argue the point anymore. There was another topic he needed to raise.

"Fine, I'll talk to the cops," he said, "but this next one is non-negotiable. If you don't do this, I drop the case. Period."

Hawkins's expression turned serious. Raine wasn't one to lay down ultimatums. Lawyers negotiated. They rarely dictated. When they did, it was serious. "Do what, Dan?"

"Get out of Seattle," Raine answered. "If Szabo didn't murder Lydia, he thinks you did. He'll come after you, and

Cindy, and Trevor. Even if he did do it, he might still come after you, because everyone will expect him to."

"Unless he wants people to know he would kill his own daughter for disloyalty," Sommers supposed.

Hawkins pointed at Sommers. "I agree with that. Also, what do you mean 'if he didn't do it'? That's our defense. You have witnesses."

"That's our current working theory," Raine countered. "And we don't have enough witnesses for it to be our defense. Not yet, anyway."

"That's why you need to talk to those cops," Hawkins quipped.

Raine didn't laugh. "Get out of town, Mike. You and Cindy and Trevor. You need to be close enough to drive back for your court hearings, but otherwise you need to be as far away as you can be."

"Canada?" Hawkins tried another joke, a transparent effort to avoid the seriousness of his family being in mortal danger.

"Too far," Raine replied, "but good idea. Doesn't Cindy have a brother in Bellingham? That's like two hundred miles from here, and only twenty from the Canadian border. If things do go south, maybe you make that sprint across the border after all."

"Yeah, Cindy's brother Tim lives in Bellingham," Hawkins confirmed. He lowered his face into a hand. "I can't stand that guy."

"Learn how," Raine told him. "And fast. You need to be out of town no later than tomorrow. Szabo knows where you live. Even one night in your house is too many."

"Okay," Hawkins agreed. "Cindy doesn't like being in the house anyway, after what happened."

"Perfect," Raine replied. "Go visit Trevor's Uncle Tim, leave me your house key, and come back for the pretrial."

Hawkins hesitated, but finally relented. He gave Raine the house key from his key ring and called his wife on his way out the door. "Hey, honey. How's your brother Tim doing?"

After he left, Sommers turned to Raine. "Were you serious about that?"

"About Szabo being a threat?" Raine replied. "Absolutely."

Sommers shook her head. "No. The part about it maybe not being Szabo. Do you think it really could have been someone else?"

Raine frowned slightly. "A defense attorney needs a good counternarrative for the jury. A story that matches the prosecutor's evidence, but lets the defendant be innocent. So far, that's Szabo. The fact that Hawkins isn't dead already makes me think Szabo might actually be guilty. But a famous person once said, 'Follow the evidence, wherever it may lead.' We need to be open to the possibility that someone other than Szabo is the murderer."

"Like who?" Sommers questioned.

Raine shrugged. "I don't know yet. But I need to figure it out before the trial starts."

12

Raine decided to talk to the officers who worked off-duty at Hawkins's fatal fundraiser without Sommers. She had her regular job to attend to, and he didn't expect her presence to help much anyway. They were even less likely to be candid with a witness present.

The only thing more difficult than getting the cops to say something helpful was tracking them down to talk to them in the first place. Patrol officers didn't have offices. They had cars. And those were always moving to the next call.

Luckily, Raine wasn't so averse to cops that he had burned every bridge with Seattle's Finest. So, after getting the names of the officers from Hawkins, Raine contacted a sergeant who had hired him a few years back to quietly beat his kid's speeding ticket. It wasn't so much that the sergeant owed him anything—Raine had definitely gotten paid—it was more that they had a connection outside of the often adversarial relationship between cops and lawyers.

The sergeant was only able to provide limited information: badge numbers, shift times, and precinct/patrol sectors. But that would be enough. It let Raine know roughly when and where to look, rather than driving all over the entire city looking for a patrol car in a haystack. Then it was the simple matter of tuning in to the public police scanner and listening for the officer's badge number and where he was being dispatched to.

The first cop would be Officer Jim Sokolowski, day shift, West Precinct, Queen Sector 2. That was Magnolia, Hawkins's neighborhood. An affluent sector where crime was minimal and the assignment easy. A cop could spend an entire shift doing nothing more than writing a couple of traffic tickets. That was exactly what Raine found Sokolowski doing, calling in over the scanner that he was pulling over a Lamborghini SUV for speeding on Thorndyke Avenue. Raine didn't even know Lamborghini made an SUV.

There was a predictable rhythm to a traffic stop. Violation, lights and siren, pull over, initial contact, license and insurance, wait, ticket issued, released, drive away. It was during this last part that the officer took a few minutes to sit in their car, log the infraction, and write the narrative that would be used in court if the Lamborghini owner decided to contest the ticket. Those few minutes weren't something a typical driver would know about, having already driven away. But Raine knew about them. And that's when he struck.

"Officer Sokolowski?" Raine tapped on the passenger side window.

Sokolowski's head jerked up from his dash-mounted computer. His hand instinctively went to his sidearm. Probably a fair reaction in his line of work.

"I'm Dan Raine. I'm an attorney," Raine continued, hoping the additional information might move the officer's hand away from his firearm. "I represent Judge Michael Hawkins. Do you have a few moments to talk with me about what happened at his home?"

Sokolowski's wide eyes relaxed slightly. His hand remained hovering over his hip. "The murder?" he asked.

Raine recognized Sokolowski as the cop who hadn't waved back to him at the fundraiser. He estimated Sokolowski's age as mid-thirties, although it could be hard with cops. They had a stressful job, but also exercised like crazy, so there were counteracting forces of aging. He had thick, sandy blond hair that matched the thick blond mustache covering his upper lip. That arm hovering over his handgun was thick and muscular, with an already blurry tattoo of an anchor.

"Yes," Raine confirmed. "Judge Hawkins said he hired you to work off-duty security that night. I'm hoping you might have seen something that might help me prove he's innocent."

Sokolowski frowned, but finally relaxed his arm. "He didn't look very innocent standing over the victim with the murder weapon at his feet."

"You should have seen him when I walked in," Raine joked. "He was still holding the gun. Do you have three minutes? I have a job to do. Just like you."

Sokolowski thought for a moment, then shrugged. "Sure. Why not? But I don't think I'm going to be very much help to you."

"The truth is always helpful," Raine offered, even if he didn't necessarily believe it.

Sokolowski didn't seem particularly convinced either. He

chuckled, then pulled himself out of the driver's seat and met Raine on the other side of his patrol car. He leaned against it and crossed his sinewy forearms. Gray clouds were forming overhead, dimming the afternoon sunlight. "Okay, counselor. I'm ready for your questions. Fire away."

"First question," Raine began. "What were your duties that night?"

"Pretty simple," Sokolowski answered. "Patrol the perimeter. Look for anyone trying to get in without being on the guest list. Things like that. Judge Hawkins said he was worried about some bad guys crashing the party. He didn't say who, but he seemed really serious about it. I guess I know why now."

"Why?" Raine followed up.

"Why?" Sokolowski laughed. "Emil Szabo, that's why. Everybody knows he's into some shady shit. I just didn't know the judge was in it too."

"He wasn't," Raine felt obligated to say.

"Okay," Sokolowski accepted unconvincingly. "I'm just saying, it might have been nice to know who he thought was going to crash the party. I might have been a little more on guard."

"What do you mean?" Raine questioned.

"I thought we might get some protesters or something like that," Sokolowski answered. "Some forlorn mother whose son was going to prison after Hawkins sentenced him. Not a crime boss coming to protect his daughter."

Raine cocked his head. "Protect?"

"Well, yeah," Sokolowski answered. "His daughter was the murder victim, right? I heard the judge's son got mixed up with her and ended up in some of that shady shit I was talking about earlier. Sounds to me like Hawkins planned to kill her that night and wanted to make sure her old man didn't show up to stop him."

Raine just stared at the cop for several seconds. A raindrop struck his cheek.

"What?" Sokolowski asked after a few awkward seconds.

"That's even worse than what the prosecutor is arguing," Raine answered. "That's not a murder of passion. That's premeditation. And it's believable."

"Sure is," Sokolowski confirmed. "I'm guessing that doesn't help you, counselor."

Raine shook his head. "No. Not at all." Another few raindrops splattered on the sidewalk next to his feet. "Did you see Szabo that night? We have other witnesses who said they saw someone who matched his description."

"What's the description?" Sokolowski asked.

"White male," Raine answered. "Late fifties to early sixties. Gray hair. Nice suit. Expensive car."

Sokolowski laughed again and shook his head. "Sorry, counselor, but that's half the people I saw that night. The other half were the women with them, and they all looked the same too."

Raine had known the cops wouldn't be helpful. He didn't think they would be so damaging. And Sokolowski was only the first of two. "What about after the gunshot? You ran toward the house, right? Did you see anyone leaving?"

"Did I see any of those old rich folks fleeing after they heard a gunshot?" Sokolowski asked with a grin. "Yeah, all of them. Except your guy. He was standing over a dead girl."

At least Raine knew how Sokolowski would come across on the witness stand. Devastating.

"I think that's all the questions I have for you now, Officer," Raine said. The raindrops were settling into a solid drizzle. "I'm sure I'll see you again at the trial."

"Trial?" Sokolowski questioned as he pushed himself off his patrol car. "The judge isn't taking a deal?"

Raine shrugged. "I don't think the prosecutor will be offering one."

Sokolowski nodded. "Yeah, neither would I. Killing a girl like that in cold blood? Sorry to say it, but he doesn't deserve a deal."

Raine just nodded in acknowledgement. The jury was likely to feel the same way.

THE SECOND OFF-DUTY cop Hawkins had hired the night of the murder was Corporal Nick Turner. A corporal was basically just a patrol officer who showed enough competence, or had enough experience, that they could step in for the shift sergeant if necessary. It was rarely necessary, but Turner got two stripes on his sleeve and an extra step in the pay grid. It was good work if you could get it.

Turner worked Southwest Precinct, Waterfront Sector 2. Everyone else called that Alki, another relatively low-crime neighborhood. Alki was the beach at the north end of West Seattle, a peninsula separated from downtown by the Duwamish River and Elliott Bay. On a nice day, the beach would be covered in volleyball games and sandcastles, the sidewalk running the length of the beach filled with bicyclists and inline skaters.

By the time Raine drove almost the entire length of the city from Magnolia to Alki, a solid rain had chased everyone away. Everyone except for the teenagers Turner had just arrested for trying to shoplift from one of the tourist shops that dotted the beach front. Raine heard Turner's badge number on the call-out on the police scanner. He arrived just as the culprits were being stuffed into the patrol car of one of the officers who had responded to assist.

Raine walked toward the collection of police officers and called out, "Officer Turner," to see which one would respond.

Turner was standing just inside the store, still speaking with the shopkeeper. He turned to Raine and raised his chin slightly. "May I help you, sir?" His hand also moved slightly toward his gun belt.

Raine slowed his gait, lest Turner appraise him as a threat. "I'm attorney Dan Raine. I represent Judge Michael Hawkins. I was hoping I could ask you a few questions."

Turner's brow creased deeply. "This isn't a good time. I'm in the middle of a call."

"Looks like the call is almost over." Raine jerked a thumb at the apprehended shoplifters locked in the patrol car. "I can wait."

Turner sighed. He was taller and thinner than Sokolowski, but still had a muscular frame under his blue uniform and yellow stripes. He turned back to the shopkeeper. "Please wait here, sir. This won't take me long."

Raine would have appreciated the preference Turner seemed to be showing him, but he knew Turner's actual calculus was that it would take less time to get rid of Raine than it would be to conclude the theft call.

Turner walked straight up to him, extended a palm at Raine's chest, and backed him all the way to the sidewalk. "What the hell do you think you're doing?" the cop demanded.

"My job?" Raine offered. "I represent Judge Hawkins and he's—"

"I know what he is," Turner interrupted. "He's charged with murder. And if he's lucky, he'll live to see the inside of a prison cell."

"That doesn't sound very lucky to me," Raine replied.

"He killed Emil Szabo's daughter," Turner hissed in a lowered voice. "I can't believe he isn't already dead. And I'm not about to put myself in the ground next to him by being seen talking to his lawyer."

"He didn't—" Raine began to protest.

"Save it," Turner cut him off. "I know what I saw and I know what everyone but you thinks. Hawkins killed that girl, and he's going to pay. His whole family is going to pay. But mine isn't. You need to leave. Now."

Turner didn't wait for Raine to agree. He spun on his heel and marched back to the entrance of the store.

Raine stood in the rain watching after him. He thought of his ex-wife, Natalie, and hoped his own boys were somewhere safe.

13

Jason and Jordan were with Raine the very next weekend. He could personally keep them safe for at least those couple of days. Natalie offered to drop them off at Raine's apartment building on her way out of town for a weekend trip. Raine didn't ask her where she was going, and he definitely didn't ask who she was going with. He knew he didn't get to have questions for her anymore—they were divorced—but he decided he did have something to tell her.

"Hey, Dad! What's for dinner? Race ya' to the elevator, Jace! Winner picks the pizza toppings!" Raine's younger son, Jordan, shouted all of that in one breath as he spilled out of the back seat of his mom's car and ran past Raine into the apartment building lobby.

Jason, the older one, firmly in his teenage years, slowly climbed out of the front passenger seat, his eyes somehow both rolled into his skull and glued to his phone. "I never agreed to pizza," he grumbled at no one in particular, and certainly not his father, whom he completely ignored on his way into the building.

"Good luck." Natalie laughed, with a wave through the passenger window. "You're sure you can get them to school Monday morning? You said you could do that this time."

"Well, actually, Nat," Raine started. He stepped up to the passenger window and leaned down to talk to her. "Do you have a minute? There's something I wanted to tell you."

"You know, Dan, I kinda don't have a minute," Natalie replied brusquely. The evening sun glinted off her brown hair. "That was the whole point of dropping them off instead of waiting for you to come pick them up."

"Right, but—" Raine tried.

"Rush hour." Natalie gestured vaguely toward the road and the traffic on it. "I need to go before it gets even worse."

"Hold on, Nat." Raine leaned onto the car. "It'll just take a second. It's about one of my cases."

"One of your cases?" Natalie laughed again, but not warmly. "I'm your ex-wife, Dan, not your paralegal."

"No, it's just," Raine tried to explain, "it's about the boys."

"Oh, no, Dan." Natalie wagged a finger at him. "You are not dumping them back on me again. Not this weekend. I told you I have plans. If this is your way of trying to sabotage my relationship with—"

"Okay, okay," Raine interjected, raising a hand at her. He didn't want to hear the name of whoever she was spending the weekend with. "Never mind. I'm not trying to sabotage anything."

A car pulled up behind Natalie's and honked. She was in a loading zone, but there was a three-minute limit, and she was blocking the traffic that wanted to join her in fleeing the city for the weekend.

"Sure, Dan," Natalie replied. "Look, I have to go. Whatever it is you wanted to tell me, I'm sure you can handle it by yourself. You were always good at that."

Raine grimaced at the final dig before Natalie put the car in drive and pulled away. It was nice to be reminded of why they had gotten divorced. But he decided to let her be right about one thing. He was good at handling things by himself.

He turned around and could see his boys through the glass of the apartment building doors. They were already arguing about something. Probably those pizza toppings. It was time to handle that problem by himself, too.

14

Raine kept his boys safe for the weekend, made sure they got to school on time, then got back to work. Hawkins's case was proceeding apace, and there was work to be done.

Raine received and reviewed the police reports, then started preparing for the pretrial conference. The pretrial was always two weeks after the arraignment, and was the first opportunity for the lawyers to negotiate intelligently about the case. Offers and counteroffers, persuasion and posturing, all occurring in a conference room outside the courtroom. If a deal was reached, the case would be set for a plea and sentencing hearing. If no deal could be reached, the case would be set for trial. Absent some unusual circumstance, the only thing the judge at the pretrial did was sit in chambers all morning and sign off on the scheduling order the lawyers prepared after their conference.

Hawkins's case had unusual circumstances.

So unusual, in fact, that the local judge sitting in chambers signing those scheduling orders would do so while a different judge, from a different county and assigned solely to the case of *The State of Washington v. Michael Hawkins*, would take the bench and call the case, if for no other reason than for introductions. The conference between the attorneys would still occur first, if only to be able to inform the visiting judge that no settlement had been reached and to request a trial date be scheduled. That would all be on the record in open court, which meant Hawkins could hide from the media in the courthouse lobby while Raine and Alexander discussed the case, but he would eventually have to come upstairs and face the cameras. His reward for driving two hours from Bellingham.

"I'll text you when you need to come up," Raine told him after a brief meeting in the lobby. "In the meantime, if any reporter spots you, do not talk to them."

"I'm not an idiot, Dan," Hawkins replied. "I know better than to talk to anyone but you about the case. Attorney-client privilege."

Raine cocked his head. "What about Cindy? You can hardly avoid talking to your spouse about the biggest thing in your lives right now, can you?"

"Don't worry." Hawkins smiled slightly. "Marital privilege. Nothing I say to either of you can be used against me in court."

"Just make sure Trevor doesn't overhear," Raine warned. "Privileges are waived if you let a third party overhear."

"I know the law." Hawkins tapped his chest. "Judge Michael Hawkins, remember?"

"How could I forget?' Raine replied. "That's why I'm solo now. And you're solo until I finish talking with Alexander. Stay down here, stay out of sight, and don't talk to anyone."

"Aye, aye," Hawkins agreed with a salute.

Raine appreciated the agreement, if not the excessive gesture that accompanied it.

"Get me a sweet deal," Hawkins added as Raine turned toward the elevators. "I'll plead guilty to a misdemeanor. Maybe disorderly conduct."

"I doubt that will be on the table," Raine called back over his shoulder, "but I'll see what I can do."

As soon as the elevator doors opened on the floor of the pretrial conference, Raine was accosted by the lights and lenses of a half dozen cameras in his face.

"Is that him?"

"That's him!"

"That's the judge's lawyer!"

"What's his name?"

"Doesn't matter. We can get it later."

"Sir, sir! Why did he do it?"

"Yes, why did the judge kill his son's girlfriend?"

"Was it some kind of sick love triangle?"

"What's your plan to win the case?"

"Is he going to get away with it?"

Raine raised his hands to gesture for them to back up enough to let him step off the elevator. He didn't particularly want to talk to the media. He especially didn't want to talk about fictitious incestuous love triangles. But he also knew that he had a job to do, that part of that job was swaying the opinions of any potential jurors, and that those potential jurors, whoever they might be, could end up watching the evening news that night.

Moreover, he knew Alexander wouldn't speak with the reporters. There was an extra ethical rule only for criminal prosecutors which prohibited them from saying anything to the media other than to confirm the defendant and the charges. Raine had a structural advantage when it came to tainting the jury pool. He wouldn't be doing his job if he didn't exploit that, at least a little.

"Thank you for all of those excellent questions," Raine boomed in an announcer's voice. "What I can tell you is this: Judge Hawkins is innocent, and he looks forward to his day in court. This tragic murder was committed by someone else, someone as yet unknown to law enforcement, but whose identity will soon be revealed. And when it is, Judge Hawkins will be exonerated. More importantly, justice will be served. Thank you."

Raine waved to the cameras, then slid down the hallway to a chorus of additional questions shouted at his back. He waved again over his shoulder but didn't turn around. He had given them their soundbite. They would have to select from his statement, not stammering answers to shockingly dumb questions. And anyway, he had a court date to get to.

The pretrials were conducted in a large room everyone called 'The Pit.' Back in the day, it had been far more pit-like, with no windows, dim lights, and poor ventilation. A few hours of being filled with anxious attorneys, and the place smelled like a college locker room at halftime. Since then, renovations had made the room brighter, cooler, and better ventilated, but there were still no windows, and it was still packed with attorneys.

Raine entered and began looking for Alexander among the crowd. He had arrived a few minutes after the scheduled start time, in part because of the talk with Hawkins downstairs, but also intentionally so. He knew from reputation that Alexander would be punctual. Arriving after the start time meant Alexander could wait for him, not vice versa.

Sure enough, the prosecutor was seated in the far corner,

at one of the few tables littered across the room. Most attorneys had to stand, but not Alexander the Great. Even if he hadn't arrived so early as to have his choice of seats, all he would have needed to do was walk up to whatever young prosecutor had beaten him there, and the chair would be his. Raine walked up. Alexander didn't stand.

"Mr. Raine," he greeted his opponent. "I assume this won't take long. Is Judge Hawkins willing to plead guilty as charged to murder in the first degree?"

"He is not," Raine confirmed.

"As I suspected." Alexander then pushed himself to his feet. "Neither am I willing to reduce the charges. Shall we meet our judge and set the trial date, then?"

"Sure," Raine agreed. "The sooner we try this case, the sooner Judge Hawkins can get back on the bench."

Alexander smiled slightly at Raine's bravado. He didn't reply to it. Instead, he turned and led the way to the courtroom connected to the Pit. It was mostly empty. A court reporter and bailiff sat at their workstations below where the judge would sit when a case was ready to be put on the record. Two attorneys stood in a far corner talking in whispers, discussing a case, or weekend plans, or why there were so many cameras in the back of the gallery on the other side of the security glass. A bored-looking jail guard stood by the door to the holding cells, for the rare case that an in-custody defendant actually needed to be brought before the judge.

"Mr. Alexander," the bailiff greeted the prosecutor. She didn't greet Raine. "Is your case ready? Judge Wooten has been waiting."

"What county is the judge from?" Raine spoke up.

"Pierce County," was the answer.

Only one county south, but a world away. Tacoma was

the biggest city and county seat. Raine could count on one hand the number of times he'd been to the Pierce County courthouse. They didn't even call it a courthouse. It was the 'County-City Government Office Building' or something equally unmajestic he couldn't quite remember.

"Judge Wooten isn't a big fan of Seattle," the bailiff continued. "Good luck."

Raine frowned. There were some prominent citizens from Pierce County who had a chip on their shoulders about Tacoma being the little brother to Seattle. That was part of why Raine didn't take many cases down there. A Seattle attorney was likely to be 'hometowned', the term lawyers used for being harangued about arcane local procedures and losing rulings they should have won because opposing counsel was a local attorney. He wondered whether Hawkins being a fellow judge would outweigh him being a Seattle judge.

"I just need to let my client know to come to the courtroom," Raine informed the bailiff. He jabbed a thumb at the media-filled gallery. "He didn't want to sit with the reporters."

The bailiff nodded but didn't offer any comment on Raine's explanation. "Let me know when he's arrived."

Raine agreed and turned away to send a text to Hawkins.

> Ready. Come to the courtroom. Walk past the reporters. Do not pass Go. Do not forfeit $500k.

A few seconds later, Hawkins ignored Raine's dark humor and replied with a simple:

> K.

It took several minutes before Hawkins had ascended the elevator, traversed the gauntlet of reporters, and ignored the questions being shouted at him while he waited for the bored guard to unlock the door into the secure front of the courtroom.

"Who's the judge?" was his first question. Hawkins was far more likely to know the judges outside of King County, from judicial conferences and general professional networking.

"Wooten," Raine answered. "From Pierce."

Hawkins's expression fell. "Shit."

"All rise!" the bailiff called out before Raine could follow up. "The King County Superior Court is now in session, The Honorable Frank Wooten, visiting judge, presiding."

"Not a good draw?" Raine ventured in a hushed voice.

Hawkins shook his head. "It could be worse," he whispered back, "but not much."

Judge Frank Wooten stepped out from chambers and stood atop the bench, pausing to survey the courtroom before sitting down.

Raine thought he seemed gratified to be presiding over Hawkins. He wondered if there was some bad blood between them. Judges weren't known for getting along well with their peers. Each of them was independently elected; no one was anyone else's boss. Compromises could be few and ill will high. The courts took their name from their history of the monarch holding court and deciding subjects' controversies, before eventually delegating that duty to what would become modern judges. You could take the judges away from the palace, but you couldn't take the palace intrigue from the judges.

For his part, Judge Wooten looked more mountain cabin

than gilded castle. He had a barely tamed head of thick gray hair, a bushy gray mustache that extended down to his chin, leathery skin, and thick glasses in front of piercing blue eyes. Large, yellowing teeth were visible as he ordered with a satisfied smile, "Please be seated."

Everyone in the gallery sat down again, but there weren't actually chairs for the parties. That particular courtroom was for quick scheduling issues, not lengthy testimonial hearings or trials. Attorneys were encouraged to speak and split.

Raine, Alexander, and Hawkins stepped forward to the bar in front of the judge.

Wooten nodded down at them. "Counselors," he greeted Raine and Alexander. Then, another nod to Hawkins, "Mike."

Raine supposed it must be humiliating for Hawkins to have a fellow judge presiding over him. Thankfully, Hawkins refrained from answering with a, 'Frank,' and instead offered only a silent nod.

Raine wondered why they bothered bringing in a visiting judge if that judge knew Hawkins as well as any of the local ones. Appearances, Raine supposed. But everyone knew appearances could be deceiving.

"This is the matter of *The State of Washington versus Michael Hawkins*," Judge Wooten announced for the record. "Could both attorneys please state their names for the record, please? I am acquainted with the defendant, but not with the local Seattle bar, I'm afraid."

"John Alexander, on behalf of the State," Alexander introduced himself.

"Ah, yes." Wooten nodded. "I've heard of you."

It was Raine's turn. "Daniel Raine, on behalf of the defendant, Michael Hawkins."

Wooten frowned thoughtfully for several seconds, then shook his head. "No, I haven't heard of you. Are you a public defender? You're not a public defender, are you? Not on a judge's salary, I should hope."

"I'm a private attorney," Raine confirmed. "Mr. Hawkins has retained me on this case."

Wooten nodded several more times as those ice blue eyes looked Raine up and down. "I'll look forward to seeing how that decision plays out for Judge Hawkins. Now then, have the parties reached a resolution, which seems highly doubtful to me, or will we be setting the case for trial?"

"We have not reached a resolution, Your Honor," Alexander confirmed. "The parties are requesting the Court schedule the case for trial."

"That is correct, Your Honor," Raine agreed.

Wooten nodded. "I note that Judge Hawkins managed to post bail. I assume we'll be setting this in a year or two?"

"No, Your Honor," Raine answered. "We are requesting a trial date within the speedy trial rule time limits."

Judge Wooten's eyebrows lowered together. "You want a trial within ninety days?"

"Well, the rule is ninety days from arraignment," Raine responded, "and the arraignment was two weeks ago. So, I guess we want a trial within seventy-six days."

"You don't think the State can be ready that fast, is that it?" Wooten questioned. "I have to tell you, Mr. Raine, I've read the factual summary in the declaration for probable cause. I think they'll be ready in seventy-six days. I think they're probably ready now."

"I appreciate the Court's concern, Your Honor," Raine

said in a tone that made clear he did not appreciate the Court's concern at all. "We have concerns of our own. Not the least of which is getting this case behind Judge Hawkins as soon as possible so he can return to his duties as a judge of this court."

"Be careful what you wish for, Mr. Raine," Wooten warned. "As soon as possible might mean a conviction."

"I'm aware of the system, Your Honor," Raine replied. "Just as I'm aware of the speedy trial rule. The defense demands a trial within ninety days of arraignment."

Judge Wooten stuck out a thoughtful, perhaps even impressed, lower lip and nodded several times. Then he turned to Alexander. "What say you, Mr. Prosecutor? Can you be ready in seventy-six days?"

"As the Court suggested," Alexander responded, "the State is ready now. We will be just as ready in seventy-six days. We have no objection to setting the trial within the time constraints Mr. Raine demands."

"So be it, then," Judge Wooten practically laughed. "Trial will begin exactly ten weeks from today. Seventy days, just to give ourselves a little cushion. I will preside over the trial, the remaining preliminary hearings, and any pretrial motions that may be brought before either party." He grinned, revealing those large, yellow teeth again. "Should be fun."

Wooten banged the gavel and retired back to whatever chambers he was borrowing while visiting the courthouse.

Raine told Hawkins to leave the courthouse as quickly as possible. He wanted to talk to Alexander a bit more before calling it a pretrial, but there was no reason for Hawkins to stay. And Hawkins wasn't interested in sticking around anyway. Every moment he stood in court as a defendant instead of a judge was another moment of humiliation.

Once Hawkins departed to push past the cameras, Raine turned his attention to Alexander, who had already retreated back into the Pit. Raine pushed through the attorneys assembled within and caught the prosecutor just before he exited into the hallway.

"Do you have a few moments longer?" Raine asked, reaching out to grab hold of Alexander's shoulder. It was unexpectedly muscular under his suit coat. "I have an alternative to a rushed trial date."

"The rushed trial date you insisted on?" Alexander turned around to answer, shrugging off Raine's grip. "Do tell."

"I think you should consider dismissing the case," Raine dared to suggest. "At least temporarily, while the police conduct additional investigation."

Alexander blinked at him. "Is that a serious request?"

"Dead serious," Raine replied, "if you can excuse that turn of phrase for a murder case."

Alexander frowned ever so slightly. But he didn't say no. "Do you have any specific reason why I should do that, or is it just a general wish you have because you're the defense attorney and every defense attorney wants their case dismissed?"

"I do have specific reasons," Raine answered. "But I'll be honest, John. I'm not sure if you're ready to hear them."

Alexander's frown slowly faded, replaced by an expression of boredom. "I assure you, Dan, I'm ready to hear whatever you have to say, and to react accordingly. If you have a reason I should dismiss what appears to be an iron-clad case of murder by a sitting judge, then by all means, tell me. If not, then let's get ready for trial. Your choice."

That was the rub. It was Raine's choice whether to divulge what he had learned so far. And it was a difficult choice to make, one that hinged largely on the personality and professionalism of the prosecutor. It was standard procedure for a defense attorney to do some independent investigation. It would be malpractice not to. Not all of those investigations turned up useful information. In fact, more often than not, the investigation would simply confirm the client's guilt, and maybe uncover even more evidence of it.

But every now and again, the defense investigation would turn up information that could cast real doubt on the defendant's guilt. Not strong enough to fully exonerate the defendant, but something that would give the jury pause, and in turn might give the prosecutor pause as well. It was that sort of information that Raine possessed: Emil Szabo had, probably, been seen at the scene of the murder and had, possibly, an independent motive for the murder. Raine had to guess what Alexander would do with that information.

When presented with exculpatory evidence, a prosecutor had roughly two general courses of action. The first, and most common, was to react adversely to the information. File a motion to suppress it. Direct the cops to find additional evidence to contradict it. Prepare to attack it and delegitimize it in front of the jury, regardless of how true it might be. That was the danger in providing such information at the pretrial conference, when the prosecutor would have time to discredit or even bury the information, as opposed to springing it on them mid-trial when it would be too late to do anything about it.

The alternative was that a good, ethical, justice-seeking

prosecutor would accept adverse evidence as presented and change their appraisal of the defendant's guilt, perhaps even to the point of dismissing the case. It was the prisoner's attorney's dilemma.

"What would you say if I told you," Raine said, "that another person was responsible for Lydia Szabo's murder?"

"I would say," Alexander answered, "prove it."

Raine nodded at the answer. It was fair. But he didn't have actual proof. Not yet.

"You know what, Mr. Raine?" Alexander took a step toward the exit. "Perhaps you're right. I think I'm not ready to hear your reasons, if only because you don't have them figured out quite yet. I can assure you that I'm not interested in prosecuting an innocent man. I can also assure you that it will take a lot of evidence—not conjecture but evidence—to convince me that Michael Hawkins is innocent."

Raine appreciated the honesty. And the opening. "What kind of evidence?"

"I rather think that's up to you," Alexander answered. "I have no idea what you're going on about because you haven't told me. You will have to decide what type of evidence and how much. But I can suggest you start with the basics: motive, means, and opportunity. Give me convincing evidence of all three of those for a different suspect, and we can have a productive conversation."

"That will take me a little more time," Raine admitted.

"I would think so," Alexander replied. "You better hurry."

15

"Means is settled," Raine said to Sommers when they met the next day to continue their investigation. His conference room again. Laura's coffee again. "It was Hawkins's gun. We can't get around that."

"Did the cops confirm it was Hawkins's gun, then?" Sommers asked.

"Yeah," Raine had to admit. "I got the ballistics report from the crime lab. The bullet was a little deformed from bouncing around inside Lydia's skull—"

"Gross." Sommers wrinkled her nose at the information.

"I suppose so," Raine agreed. "Anyway, they compared the bullet the medical examiner extracted from her skull to bullets they test-fired from Hawkins's gun after they seized it. They were all fired from the same gun."

"What about opportunity?" Sommers asked.

"The valets and the caterer's kid all said Szabo was there that night," Raine answered.

"He was there. He went inside the house."

"That leaves motive," Sommers said. "What could possibly have been his motive for murdering his own daughter?"

"I'm sure it had something to do with whatever she wanted to tell me that night," Raine answered.

"What do you think it was?" Sommers asked.

"I'm not sure," Raine admitted. "I wish I did. But if I had to guess, I'd say it had something to do with her father's criminal activities. Maybe something she couldn't stomach anymore. Something so bad, we could use it to get Trevor and Hawkins out from under her father's thumb."

"That's a big guess," Sommers replied. "How do we prove any of that?"

"We need to see what Szabo actually does to make all of his money," Raine answered. "Up to now, it's been all whispers and innuendo. We need to see it with our own eyes."

"How do we do that?" Sommers questioned.

Raine set down his coffee and grinned. "Come out back."

"Whose car is this?" Sommers asked when Raine led her to the several-year-old gray Toyota Camry in the parking lot behind Raine's office. The sky was heavy, but the rain hadn't started yet.

"I rented it," Raine answered. "We need a car so average-looking as to be invisible."

"For what?" Sommers questioned, but then her eyes lit up. "Wait. Are we going to tail someone? That's the phrase, right? Tail someone?"

"It might have been the phrase at some point," Raine allowed, "at least on television. But yes, we're going to follow Szabo. And we really don't want him to know we're following him."

Sommers's grin faded. "Szabo?"

"You don't have to do this," Raine gave her the out. "It doesn't take two of us to tail him. I can do it alone."

But Sommers raised her gaze and regained her usual confident smile. "And let you have all the fun? No way."

Raine smiled as well. He'd feel better with some company, especially someone who could get him to hit the brakes, literally, if he got too reckless.

"I'll drive," he said.

"Why?"

"It's my case," Raine answered reflexively, and a bit unconvincingly. They were supposed to be partners. "And because I'm the only one insured under the rental agreement."

Sommers agreed that second reason was valid. She thought for a moment. "We should wear hats."

RAINE SAT in the driver's seat, a black San Francisco Giants hat pulled low over his eyes. Sommers wore a wide-brimmed hat that matched her outfit perfectly, of course. "Are you sure this is where he lives?"

Sommers smiled. "I am, although it took some digging. Somebody like Szabo is careful not to use his home address on any official documents that might be available to the public."

"So, how do you know it?" Raine asked.

"There's one time when you have to provide your home address," Sommers answered. "Deliveries. You can't have your *prik khing* delivered if the local Thai restaurant doesn't have your home address."

"You know what he orders for takeout?" Raine questioned.

"I know where he orders takeout from," Sommers answered. "One of the biggest categories of commercial real estate is restaurants. I've helped a lot of restauranteurs secure their buildings. I only had to cash in a few favors to track down where 'Emil S.' ordered his favorite Thai food from. And more importantly, where it was delivered to."

Raine had to smile. "Are you ever going to run out of favors you can cash in?"

"Not any time soon," Sommers answered. "I've banked a lot of favors as the number one commercial real estate agent in Seattle, Downtown core and First Hill."

"So where does Emil Szabo live?" Raine asked. "Downtown or First Hill?"

"Neither," Sommers answered. "He lives in a gated community in the Leschi neighborhood. But his favorite Thai place is on First Hill."

"You have an address?" Raine asked, finally starting the car. The engine struggled against the turn of the key, and the wipers squeaked across the raindrop-dotted windshield.

"Yes, but we won't get that close," Sommers answered. "Head for Leschi. I know where we can park and see if he ever leaves."

"THERE!" Sommers called out far too loudly as she pointed at the black sedan exiting the gates of the exclusive neighborhood where Emil Szabo lived. "That's him! I think that's him. That has to be him."

Raine, who had been fighting off the urge to steal a quick

nap as they sat far too long in the rain, parked in the bend of a winding side street near the subdivision gates, sat up sharply at Sommers's shout. "Why does it have to be him?" he questioned.

"It's probably him," Sommers amended her claim. "Let's say it's him. I'm so bored."

"Okay. Why do you think it's him?" Raine asked, but he started the car again. He was pretty bored too.

"The car," Sommers answered. "It's an Aston Martin. A fancy black sedan."

"Just like Simone said." Raine signaled his turn. "Okay. Let's see where the car goes. Maybe it's that Thai place he likes."

"That's his delivery place, Dan, not dine-in," Sommers chided. "Try to keep up."

RAINE DID KEEP UP—WITH the black Aston Martin. But from a distance, lest they be noticed, although the steady rain provided additional cover. The Aston Martin made its way to the freeway, heading southbound for a short distance before exiting into the Georgetown neighborhood. Raine took the same exit, confirmed their direction, and eased up on the gas.

"Why are you slowing down?" Sommers asked.

Raine pointed ahead. "He's turning into that parking lot on the left. He has to wait for the traffic to clear. I don't want to get too close."

But the oncoming traffic was heavy and the Aston Martin had to wait too long to make the turn. Raine had to drive past—he could hardly stop in the middle of the street. They would have to turn around and double back. By the time they returned, their target had completed the turn and parked. The car was empty. The occupants had gone inside.

Raine turned into the parking lot for a liquor store across the street. He backed into a parking spot with an unobstructed view of the sleek black sedan and the business it was parked in front of.

"The Peony Spa," Sommers read the name of the business out loud. "He's getting a massage?"

"I doubt that very much," Raine replied.

"Is anything happening?" Sommers squinted through the rain. "Nothing's happening."

"Not yet," Raine agreed with a frown. "Not where we can see anyway."

"What do you think is happening where we can't see?"

Raine's frown deepened. "Something bad. Something I hope isn't happening. Maybe the something Lydia wanted to tell me about."

After several more minutes, a woman stepped out of the spa and stood under the awning above the front door. She was young and slight. She hugged herself against the cold and lit a cigarette. Raine could guess she was one of the masseuses, taking a break from the distasteful tasks that filled her day. But there was no rest for those who served the wicked for a $20 tip and the decaying promise of a better life in a new country.

Suddenly, the woman's smoke break was cut short by a visibly agitated Emil Szabo, who stormed out of the front door and grabbed the small woman by the hair at the back of her neck.

"Oh my God!" Sommers shouted. "We have to do something."

Raine's hand was already on the door handle, but three things stopped him from jumping out of the car and rushing across the street to defend the woman. The first was the large bodyguard who emerged from the business behind Szabo. The second was that it would blow their cover and undo what they were trying to do to help Hawkins avoid dying in prison. The third was that Szabo let the woman go almost as soon as he had grabbed her, shoving her away and sending her stumbling into the wall as he shook his fist and shouted at her.

He continued to berate the woman, who cowered against his words and anger. After what seemed like too long a time, an older woman emerged from the business and took up the role of peacemaker. Her body language was deferential to Szabo even as she wrapped an arm around the younger woman and led her inside. A moment later, it was just Szabo and his bodyguard on the sidewalk. A few moments after that, they were no longer alone.

A police cruiser turned from Michigan Street into the parking lot and rolled to a stop in front of the spa.

"Oh good," Sommers said. "Someone called the police."

Raine wasn't so sure. The car's lights weren't flashing. It didn't look like a callout. Any doubts Raine had that they were witnessing something other than an officer protecting and serving were dispelled when that officer emerged from his patrol car and shook Szabo's hand.

"Sokolowski," Raine hissed. He immediately recognized the blond hair and mustache, even from across the street.

"Who?" Sommers asked. "Do you know that cop?"

"Not really," Raine answered, "but Hawkins does. He hired him to do off-duty security at the fundraiser."

"The cop who was supposed to keep Szabo out," Sommers questioned,

"is friends with Szabo?"

Raine watched the two men across the street. No one was smiling. Sokolowski was averting his eyes and nodded. Their interaction wasn't one of friends. It was one of master and servant.

"Worse," Raine realized. "He's on Szabo's payroll."

16

The one thing Hawkins, Szabo, and Sokolowski had in common, the one place they had all been, was Hawkins's study. At least if Raine was right that Szabo was the real murderer. That meant Raine needed to take another look at the room to see if the police overlooked any evidence that might link Szabo to the murder, and thereby exonerate Hawkins. Raine had been working under the assumption that any such oversight would have arisen from a halfhearted investigation after settling immediately on a suspect. After what he saw in front of the Peony Spa, Raine's new theory was that the oversight was intentional. Even, to use Sokolowski's own suggestion against him, premeditated.

Raine slid Hawkins's house key into the lock and opened the front door of his friend's residence. It had been closed up for days, and the smell of death had been given a chance to pile up again. It was almost impossible to get blood out of a wood floor. Especially that thick arterial blood. The odor sent a slow chill up his spine. He was glad he'd decided to bring his handgun with him, just in case, although it probably wouldn't be of much use against ghosts.

Raine closed the door behind him and headed for the stairs. Hawkins had left on two dimmed lights in the front room and the overhead light in the upstairs hallway. It allowed for the illusion that someone was still living there, if you didn't notice it was always the same three lights. Raine's car in the driveway probably added to the impression of occupancy. He should probably come over more often to prevent Szabo from realizing Hawkins had skipped town—if he didn't know already.

Raine wondered how many more cops were on the old man's payroll. It was unlikely to be just Sokolowski. Corporal Turner? Detective Ewing? Others? Almost certainly. It made calling 911 a far less attractive option should he find himself needing help from law enforcement in the immediate future, especially with Hawkins's home being in Sokolowski's sector.

The stairs creaked under Raine's weight, something he hadn't noticed over the noise of the party the last time he'd climbed the steps. At the top of the stairs, he took a moment to recall the layout of the rooms. Hawkins's study was to the immediate right. Cindy's office was across the hall to the left. Ahead on the left was their bedroom, and ahead on the right was the guest room made from Trevor's childhood room. Raine would start in Hawkins's study, but he might as well check each of the rooms. Maybe Sokolowski tossed a piece of evidence into Cindy's office when no one was looking.

That stench of dried blood was strongest in the study. Raine wrinkled his nose against it and decided he would start with the window, if only to have an excuse to open it. He turned on the overhead light and stepped around the stain in the middle of the floor. The curtains were drawn, so he pulled them apart and opened the window. There was a nice view of the backyard. The lights in the pool weren't on, but there was a single dim light visible in Trevor's pool house apartment. Another attempt to make the property lived in, Raine supposed.

Raine turned back to the study and shoved his hands on his hips. He had no idea what he was looking for or where it might be found. The idea of starting in one corner and painstakingly examining every inch of the room was hardly appealing, but he couldn't think of an alternative. At least he'd worn comfortable clothes. He walked to the opposite corner and knelt onto the floor. He braced himself for a long night.

As it turned out, however, despite his desire to be slow and methodical, there wasn't much for Raine to linger over. Between the cops' evidence collection and the Hawkinses' housecleaning, the study floor was bare of anything other than some dust, and not much of that. It didn't take nearly as long as he'd feared to confirm there were no overlooked items of evidence in the hidden crevices of the study. He pushed himself to his feet again at the window, grateful for the fresh air blowing into the room.

He looked out the window at the yard below. It was a peaceful scene, but Raine found it bothersome. Could an old man like Szabo really have jumped out of the window without hurting himself??

He scanned the area and made a happy discovery. Affixed to the wall between the windows of Hawkins's study and the guest room was a wooden trellis, mostly covered in ivy. It probably wasn't strong enough to hold the weight of a grown adult who tried to climb up it, but it might offer an adult heading the other direction just enough support to shorten the jump to the grass below to a safe distance.

Raine reached out and grabbed the thin wooden lattice. It had partially disconnected from the wall, further supporting the theory that someone too large had tried to use it as a ladder. He gave it a shake, and when he did, he noticed a small object fall a few inches into a clump of ivy below the windowsill. Raine leaned over the ledge and carefully reached into the bundle of leaves. His fingertips found something small, hard, and round. Extracting his hand again, he held the item to the light. It was a button. A black, plastic button, with a short length of broken thread hanging from it.

"Bingo." Raine smiled at the find. Evidence.

He clutched the button in his hand and pulled himself back into the study. He shoved the plastic disk into his pants pocket and was ready to call the night a success when two small movements outside grabbed his attention. The first was a quick dimming of the light in the pool house, as if someone passed in front of the lamp. The second was the flash of metal in the hand of the otherwise nearly invisible figure in the shadows on the far side of the yard.

Raine rushed to turn off the study light and returned to the window, squinting against the dark to make out the figure bearing down on the apparently occupied pool house. One of the few walkway lights in the backyard cast a brief glow on the approaching figure, and Raine was able to confirm two things: the man definitely had a handgun, and he definitely did not have his left eye.

"Alexei," Raine hissed under his breath.

Alexei Szabo was bearing down on the pool house, and while Trevor was supposed to be in Bellingham with his parents, someone was moving around inside the pool house. That was almost certainly Trevor. And if Raine didn't do something, Trevor wouldn't be moving for long.

Raine reached under his jacket and removed his handgun from its holster. It was a simple 9 mm. No silencer or anything like that. Just a basic gun for a basic lawyer who spent a career pissing off at least half the people he encountered. It would be loud. But that was the point. He wasn't going to kill Emil Szabo's other child.

Raine pointed his gun toward the night sky and fired two shots, the discharges shattering the quiet of the otherwise peaceful evening.

The gunshots had the desired effect. Several of them. Alexei froze and looked all around at who might be shooting at him. Every dog in the neighborhood started barking. Half of the nearby houselights turned on. The neighborhood fixed its attention on the Hawkins residence. And the last thing Alexei Szabo wanted was attention. He had a very distinctive appearance. He would be identified if seen.

Raine watched as Alexei hesitated, then turned and sprinted back across the lawn. Toward the road. Away from the pool house. Away from Trevor. Hawkins's son was safe, albeit temporarily. Until Alexei Szabo returned. Or until Raine himself got his hands on the young man.

Trevor Hawkins had some explaining to do.

By the time Raine made his way downstairs and out the back door, Trevor—poor, stupid Trevor—was standing outside the pool house, looking all around and being a perfect target for Alexei should he decide to return. Raine suspected that was unlikely. Police sirens were already audible. Alexei was long gone. Raine and Trevor needed to follow suit.

"Trevor!" Raine barked at him, gun still in hand. "We need to leave. Now."

Trevor raised his hands. "Are you going to shoot me?"

Of course Raine wasn't going to shoot him. But he could tell Trevor that after he got into Raine's car. "Get in my car. It's parked in the driveway." He gestured toward the front of the house with the barrel of the gun. "I won't ask twice."

Trevor flinched and hurried around the side of the house.

Raine holstered his gun, locked the back door, and met Trevor at his car. They drove away just as the flashing lights of the approaching police cars came into view up ahead on Magnolia Boulevard.

"Did..." Trevor stammered, "did you try to kill me?"

"I just saved your life," Raine answered. "Lydia's brother was about to kill you."

Trevor's face went white. "Alexei?"

"One and the same," Raine confirmed. He steered the car through the winding curves as the street twisted from westbound to northbound. "I was upstairs investigating the crime scene when I noticed him sneaking across the backyard with a gun in his hand. He's pretty easy to recognize."

Trevor nodded, staring out the windshield. His brown curls stuck to the sweat on his forehead. "So, you shot him?"

"I didn't shoot anybody," Raine barked. "I shot in the air to scare him. And you're lucky I did."

Raine crossed Emerson Street and brought the car to a stop in the south parking lot of Discovery Park, one of the city's largest green spaces. Away from the road and the cops.

"Now it's my turn to ask the questions, Trevor," Raine announced. "Let's start with why you're not in Bellingham with your parents."

Trevor lowered his eyes. "They don't know I'm here. I told them I was going out to the movies with friends."

"Do you even have any friends in Bellingham?" Raine questioned.

"No," Trevor admitted, "but they don't know that."

"Like they don't know you drove two hours to come back to your house and almost get killed," Raine said. "Why in the world are you down here tonight?"

"I just..." Trevor closed his eyes. "I miss Lydia. I wanted to be where we used to spend the night together."

Raine pursed his lips. He supposed he could understand that. "Didn't you guys have a big argument the night she died? Did you break up or something?"

Trevor opened his eyes again and glared at Raine. "We did not break up," he practically wailed. "And it wasn't an argument. It was a disagreement."

At least Raine knew Trevor could lie to him. "It was an argument, Trev. My girlfriend and I were right outside, remember? We even talked to Lydia before you came out of the pool house. You seemed pretty upset."

"Oh, so you think I murdered Lydia?" Trevor cried out.

"I didn't say that," Raine replied. "And lower your voice. I'm right here. I can hear you. I don't want anyone else to hear us too."

"You think I murdered Lydia?' Trevor repeated in an angry whisper. "Well, I didn't. So there. It was my dad. Or her dad. Or someone else. I don't know. But it wasn't me. It wasn't me."

Raine frowned at Trevor. At everything about him. His words, his attitude, his demeanor, his emotionality. "Then why was Alexei Szabo at the house tonight? Why was he going to kill you?"

"I don't know!" Trevor's voice shot up again. "Because he's a terrible person, maybe? All of the Szabos are terrible people."

Raine waited a beat for the qualifier, but when it didn't come, he prompted, "Except Lydia, right?"

Trevor rolled his eyes. "Yes, except Lydia. Of course, except Lydia."

"Did you have some other beef with Alexei?" Raine pressed. "Isn't he the one you owed the money to? Was he coming to threaten you about that, maybe?"

Trevor thought for a moment, then nodded. "Yes, yes. That's probably it. I still owe them money."

"So, you came all the way down to Seattle," Raine summarized Trevor's explanations, "because you missed Lydia, and then coincidentally her brother shows up to kill you, but over outstanding debts and not in revenge for the murder of his sister. Is that what you're telling me?"

Trevor shrugged. "That's what I'm telling you."

"Is that what you're going to tell your parents?" Raine asked.

The color ran out of Trevor's face again. "Tell my parents? I'm not going to tell them anything. They think I'm at the movies."

"That's fine." Raine smiled. "I'll tell them for you."

"What?" Trevor gasped. "Oh no, please don't. I—"

"I kind of have to, Trevor," Raine replied. "Lawyer ethics and all that. But I'll tell you what. I'll give you a head start. I won't say anything until this time tomorrow. That gives you a day to get home and get straight with your parents. They've done a lot to protect you. The least you can do is be honest with them."

Trevor didn't reply. He just lowered his gaze again and clasped his hands together.

"Where's your car?" Raine asked.

Trevor looked up again. "I parked around the corner from the house."

Raine chuckled. "That's not suspicious at all."

"I didn't kill Lydia!" Trevor practically screamed.

"I never said you did," Raine responded after a moment. He didn't say it, but he was starting to think it.

17

Raine did not, in fact, call Hawkins the next night to snitch out his son. An adult child lying to his parents was a family matter until it obviously became something more.

Raine decided to wait until the omnibus hearing to talk to him about it. The omnibus hearing was like the pretrial conference, but more formal. The lawyers would appear in open court, and the judge would go through a checklist to ensure that everything that needed to be done was being done, so that the case could proceed to trial as scheduled. But prior to that, it was another opportunity for the prosecutor and defense to negotiate the case. Plenty of cases that failed to settle at the pretrial conference reached resolution at the omnibus after the lawyers had the opportunity to more fully prepare, and appraise, their positions.

Raine found Alexander in the Pit, again already seated at a small table in the corner. Hawkins hadn't arrived yet, but Raine expected him in time to appear before Judge Wooten. There were no cameras that day. The media had lost interest temporarily. When the actual trial began, they were sure to return, like vultures to a carcass. The Pit was also less busy than at a pretrial conference calendar. Every case had a pretrial. Only the ones that didn't settle then needed an omnibus.

"Good morning," Raine greeted Alexander as he sat down opposite him. "Any point in negotiating?"

Alexander tilted his head to the side. "That depends, Mr. Raine. Do you have any of that proof you said you were going to get me? The evidence that someone other than Judge Hawkins committed the murder he so obviously committed."

Raine frowned tightly. "I'm still working on it."

"You might want to work faster," Alexander suggested. "It's been several weeks since the pretrial, with nothing to show for your efforts, apparently. Trial is fast approaching, less than a month away now. But that's what you want, right?"

"I want an immediate dismissal," Raine answered. "Short of that, I'll take a speedy acquittal."

"I'm sure you would. I'll do my best to deny you that." Alexander stood up. "Shall we have the bailiff call for Judge Wooten? I'm sure he's anxious to be heading south again as soon as he can."

Raine wasn't so sure about that. Wooten seemed to be enjoying himself, whether because he got to lord over a fellow judge or because he could feel like a small celebrity as a visiting judge on an important case.

Raine stood as well. "Uh, let me just make sure my client is here. Parking is a bitch around the courthouse, right?"

Alexander didn't respond to the prompt. Instead, he headed for the courtroom as Raine headed for the hallway.

Once outside the Pit, he dialed Hawkins's number. But there was no answer.

"Call me when you get this, Mike," Raine left a voicemail. "You're late for the omnibus and Judge Wooten doesn't have any other cases, so he's going to notice. Hurry up and get here."

Raine reentered the Pit to find Alexander waiting for him by the entrance. "Is Judge Hawkins in the building? No cameras today, so no need to wait in the lobby."

"He's, uh, running a little late," Raine explained. "I'm sure he'll be here soon. Maybe you want to swing by your office for a bit? Check your email maybe? I can call you when he gets here."

Alexander's expression hardened slightly. "If he fails to appear today, I will ask for a warrant in the amount of five million dollars. I'll get it too. Judge Pereidas never should have set bail so low. He's probably halfway to Canada by now."

He's a lot more than halfway, Raine thought. "He's not going to fail to appear. He's just running late. Haven't you ever been late for something?"

Alexander just stared at him. Raine suspected Alexander was rarely late for anything.

"I will wait in the courtroom," Alexander informed Raine. "The judges usually give defendants a thirty-minute grace period. I will be asking for a warrant at nine thirty-one."

Raine didn't bother replying. He had nothing to say. Hawkins needed to show up, and soon, or Yu's bail money would be forfeited and he would be remanded back into custody at a bail amount he would never be able to post.

At 9:15, Raine called Hawkins again, but again there was no answer.

At 9:20, Raine searched the hallway for his client, but without success.

At 9:25, Raine texted him:

> Warrant in 5 mins. Where r u?

At 9:28, Raine dropped his shoulders and walked into the courtroom.

Judge Wooten was already on the bench, waiting for him. "Where is your client, Mr. Raine?" the judge demanded. "It's almost nine thirty."

"I'm not sure where he is, Your Honor," Raine admitted, "but I am going to ask the Court to refrain from issuing a bench warrant a little while longer. I have no reason to believe Judge Hawkins intended to miss today's court appearance. Therefore, I believe it's reasonable to conclude something unforeseen has arisen. The court rules are replete with exceptions for unforeseen circumstances."

"I will be asking for a warrant, Your Honor," Alexander put in. "It is now nine thirty, and the defendant has failed to appear for court. The Court should forfeit the bail already posted and issue a warrant in the amount of ten million dollars."

"Ten?" Raine called out. "You said five million in the Pit."

"I thought more about it," Alexander responded.

Wooten frowned. "I would prefer not to issue a warrant in this case, Mr. Raine, but your client is giving me no other choice."

Raine was about to beg for thirty more minutes when the gallery door opened and Hawkins sprinted to pound on the secure door separating the public from the front of the courtroom.

"Just in the nick of time." Wooten grinned.

Alexander frowned. "I think the Court could still forfeit the bail and raise bail to the new amount."

"I could," Judge Wooten agreed, "but I won't. He's here. Let's keep things on track for trial."

The guard unlocked the door and let Hawkins into the courtroom.

Raine rushed up to him before he stepped in front of the judge. "Where have you been?" he asked under his breath.

"There was an accident on the freeway," Hawkins answered in his own hushed tone. "Just south of Mount Vernon. It took forever to get through."

Mount Vernon was sixty miles north of Seattle, and still thirty miles closer than where Hawkins had been staying. Raine didn't think Wooten would appreciate Hawkins having moved, even temporarily, to Canada's doorstep. Especially not after the scare Hawkins had caused by his late arrival.

"Don't mention Mount Vernon," Raine whispered back. "Or Bellingham. Or anything. Let me do the talking."

"Of course," Hawkins agreed. "You're the lawyer."

"Are you ready, Mr. Raine?" Judge Wooten called out.

"We are, Your Honor," Raine answered. He marched forward with Hawkins in tow. "My client apologizes for his late arrival. Traffic."

"Traffic?" Wooten raised an eyebrow. "That's it? That's the explanation? I almost issued a warrant."

"Traffic, Your Honor," Raine repeated. "The defense is ready to proceed with the omnibus hearing."

Wooten frowned slightly, but then looked to the prosecutor. "Mr. Alexander?"

Alexander sighed, but then capitulated. "The State is ready as well, Your Honor."

"All right then," Wooten responded. He pulled a paper in front of him and raised his glasses out of the way in order to read it. "My first question is whether the parties still anticipate being ready to begin the case on the scheduled trial date. We are only three weeks away now."

"The State will be ready, Your Honor," Alexander answered.

"The defense will be ready as well, Your Honor," Raine assured.

"Okay, if you say so," the judge mumbled. He moved to the next item on the omnibus order. It was a checklist of everything that was supposed to be done by both sides to ensure the case was ready for trial. It was also a roadmap for the hearing. Wooten would take them through the checklist, then sign it and send them away until the readiness hearing on the Friday before trial, the final chance for either side to blink.

"Discovery is complete?" Judge Wooten asked without looking up from the form. "All police reports have been provided to defense? Expert reports? Crime scene photos?"

"Yes, Your Honor," Alexander answered.

"To the best of my knowledge, Your Honor," Raine hedged. "There's nothing obviously missing."

"Hmm, all right." Wooten checked off a box. He finally looked up. "What about pretrial motions? I checked the court file before I took the bench, and there are no pretrial motions filed. Will you not be filing any pretrial motions, Mr. Raine?"

Raine forced a smile. Nothing like having your professional judgment questioned.

"I mean," Judge Wooten continued, "I've reviewed the case and I didn't see any obvious issues that would lead me to believe I would suppress any of the evidence against your client. But that doesn't always stop defense attorneys from filing their motions."

Raine's smile became genuine. Nothing like having your professional judgment affirmed.

"Thank you, Your Honor," he responded. "No pretrial motions from the defense. We are ready to put the evidence, all of the evidence, to a jury."

"Fine with me." Wooten checked off another box. "That's one less day I have to drive up here. The traffic around here is terrible, as the defendant can attest to, I suppose. I will probably stay in a hotel during the trial."

Raine was unsure whether he was supposed to respond to that information. He elected not to.

They ran through the rest of the checklist and soon enough, the hearing was over. Wooten signed the omnibus order and adjourned the case until the readiness hearing, two weeks out and one week before the commencement of the trial. Alexander departed for his office without further discussion with Raine. That was fine with Raine. He needed to talk to Hawkins.

They found an empty attorney-client meeting room at the end of the hallway.

"Sorry again about being late," Hawkins began as he sat in one of the room's two chairs.

Raine waved him off. "I don't care about that," he said, remaining standing. "No damage done. Wooten didn't forfeit your bail, and he didn't issue a warrant. Just leave earlier next time. A lot earlier."

"I'll probably move back into the house for the trial," Hawkins said. "I don't want to get stuck fifty miles away when I'm supposed to be sitting in front of a jury."

Raine raised a cautionary index finger. "About that. Have you talked to Trevor?"

"Do you mean today?" Hawkins questioned. "I talk to him every day."

"I mean, did he tell you what happened at your house last week?" Raine asked.

Hawkins took a moment. "What happened? And how would he know?"

Raine sighed and finally dropped himself into the other chair. "I was at your house. So was Trevor. And so was Szabo's son, Alexei."

"What?" Hawkins gasped. "Why?"

"I think Alexei was there to kill Trevor," Raine explained. "I managed to scare him away with a couple of unexpected gunshots. I confronted Trevor about why he was there. He said he missed Lydia and wanted to go back to the apartment he shared with her, or something like that."

Hawkins's expression dropped. He'd been holding up okay, all things considered. Raine thought he might have lost a few pounds, and his shoulders seemed a little stooped, but nothing more than Raine would have expected considering the gravity of the situation he found himself in. But then, his friend's face suddenly looked very old and very tired.

"Why would Szabo want to kill Trevor?" Hawkins asked.

Raine knew the answer. They both did. But he didn't say it. "I don't know."

Hawkins nodded, his dark eyes downcast. "We have to win this trial, Dan. You have to convince the jury Szabo did it."

"I know," Raine answered. "And I will."

18

"Oh, shit. Szabo didn't do it." Sawyer shook her head. "You're in trouble."

It was several days later. Raine had invited Sawyer out for a working lunch. The lunch was at the best Mexican place within walking distance from the courthouse. The work was the impending trial in the matter of *The State of Washington versus Michael Hawkins*.

"Why do you say that?" Raine asked, although he knew the answer. He just wanted someone else to say it. A someone else who was a lawyer, and a damn good one at that.

"Test each hypothesis and work backwards," Sawyer explained. "Compare Szabo's reaction to his daughter's murder against what we would expect to happen depending on who the real killer was."

Raine nodded. "Seems reasonable." As if he hadn't already done exactly that and then called Sawyer in the hopes that he was wrong.

"Let's start with Hawkins," Sawyer suggested. "If he did

it, then Szabo probably stands back and lets the justice system run its course. He doesn't draw any additional attention to his own criminal activities, and Hawkins gets convicted and sent to prison. My guess is, Szabo has connections inside the prison system and can wait to go after Hawkins if he wants to take revenge, which he probably does. Hawkins is probably dead within a week of arriving at the prison."

"Maybe less," Raine agreed.

"Next, let's assume Szabo is the one who killed Lydia," Sawyer continued. She lifted a forkful of enchilada verde. "Maybe she really was going to tell you what you needed to expose Szabo's criminal enterprise. Maybe she told him what she was going to do and dared him to try to stop her, so he killed her. If that's the case, he doesn't need to take revenge on anyone because he's the one who did it. He still lets Hawkins take the fall for the murder—because, why not?—but on the streets, people will know he murdered his own daughter for disloyalty, and they will know not to cross him."

"Agreed." Raine nodded. He took a bite of his steak fajitas.

"Those are the two scenarios the jury will get," Sawyer went on. "Alexander will give them the one where Hawkins is the killer, and you will give them the counter-narrative that it was really Szabo."

"Yes," Raine confirmed.

"But here's the problem," Sawyer said. "In neither of those scenarios does Alexei try to murder Trevor before the trial."

Raine could only nod.

"Do you know," Sawyer asked him, "in what scenario

Alexei Szabo does try to murder Trevor Hawkins right now, regardless of the impact it might have on the trial?"

Raine did. He just didn't want to say it.

"The scenario," Sawyer answered for him, "where Trevor is the one who murdered Lydia."

Raine shook his head. "Hawkins will never let me argue that to the jury."

"That's where the evidence leads, Dan," Sawyer insisted. "And that leads to an acquittal for your client. Your job is to win the case, and that's how you win the case."

"Hawkins is not going to want to win the case if it means convicting his own child of murder," Raine returned. "No parent would."

"So, represent Trevor next and win that case too," Sawyer said. "But you can't lose a murder case because you're afraid of hurting a third party, even if that third party is your client's kid."

"He won't go for it." Raine shook his head. "He'll fire me before he lets me do that."

"So, let him fire you," Sawyer argued. "There's no dishonor in being fired for doing your job. That's not being a bad lawyer. That's having a bad client."

"He's not just a client," Raine tried to explain. "He's my friend."

Sawyer clicked her tongue and scooped up another forkful of enchilada. "Maybe that's the problem." She ate her bite, then set her fork down again. "Have you even actually talked to him about this?"

"We kind of talked around it after what happened at his house," Raine related, "but we didn't address it directly. We both knew what his answer would be."

"You think you know," Sawyer challenged, "but you

could be wrong. Maybe he'll be okay with it. Maybe he real-
izes you fight one battle at a time, and you win them one at a
time. I mean, how strong of a case can the prosecutor
present against Trevor when they already went all in against
his father and lost? The jury will see it for what it really is."

"I hope not," Raine responded. "If the jury sees what it
really is, Trevor might go down for murder."

"Talk to Hawkins," Sawyer repeated. "You have to let him
make the decisions, but he can't do that if you don't put the
choices to him honestly. After you explain it to him, I bet he
sees you're right."

Raine allowed a lopsided smile. "Maybe you're right."

Sawyer grinned broadly. "Of course I'm right."

———

SAWYER WAS NOT RIGHT.

"No way, Dan." Hawkins sprang to his feet and slapped
the conference room table. They were doing a client meeting
at Raine's office. Their old office. Just the two of them. Raine
sent Laura home for the rest of the day so they could be as
honest and as loud as they needed to be. "There is no way
we tell the jury Trevor did it."

"It's just an idea," Raine tried to calm his friend. "Some
of the evidence is starting to point that way. I wanted to see
what your thoughts were about maybe expanding our
theory of the case."

"Expand it to convict my son of murder?" Hawkins began
pacing around the room.

Raine remained seated, in an effort to exude calmness.
"No. We don't convict anybody of anything. That's the whole
point. We don't have to prove Trevor did it. Or Szabo, for that

matter. We just have to show the jury that it's reasonable to think someone else did it. If they think that, then that's reasonable doubt, even if they aren't convinced the other suspects did it either. We just need them to throw their hands up and say, 'We don't know!' That's reasonable doubt. That's an acquittal."

Hawkins stopped pacing and came to a stop directly across the table from Raine. He leaned forward and grabbed hold of either side of the chair in front of him. "Listen, Dan. I appreciate you. I really do. There's no one else I'd want defending me. And part of why I want you to be my lawyer is because you will think of stuff like this and present it to me, even though you know how I'm going to react. I admire that. I respect that. I'm grateful for that."

"Thanks, Mike," Raine felt compelled to reply.

"But you know me, Dan," Hawkins continued. "You know my family. You know what kind of husband I want to be, and you know what kind of father I want to be. I would rather die than let my only child go to prison."

"Even if he did it," Raine added. It wasn't a question.

"Even if he did it," Hawkins confirmed. "So, while I admire your imagination and your advocacy, we will not be doing anything that in any way suggests that my son murdered Lydia Szabo. And if you do, I will fire you on the spot. In front of the jury, if I have to. Is that clear?"

Raine nodded. He'd tried. "Crystal clear."

Hawkins hung his head and sighed. "Good." He looked up again. "So, now what?"

"Now," Raine offered a smile, "I guess I better find more evidence against Emil Szabo."

19

Raine thought he knew what he needed to do to implicate Emil Szabo sufficiently to craft a credible motive for the murder of his own daughter. But before he could put that plan into motion, he had a small fire to put out.

"Mr. Yu stopped by while you were out," Laura informed him after an afternoon at the courthouse attending to the cases of some of his other clients. "He left his business card."

Raine took the card from Laura. On the back was scrawled:

'Come see me. -SY.'

"Crap," Raine hissed through his teeth.

"Problem?" Laura inquired.

"More like a potential problem," Raine replied. "I just need to do a little massaging to keep a nervous bondsman from doing something rash."

"Massage, huh?" Laura replied. "That sounds nice."

"It can be. At least for the person getting the massage."

He held the card aloft. "I will be on Third Avenue, if anyone needs me, giving a massage to a screaming eagle."

"That's quite the mental image." Laura laughed.

It was nothing compared to the other mental images Raine was juggling in his head just then. But he needed to set those aside long enough to deal with Sebastian Yu. He knew what Yu could do, and he knew he could do it at any time.

He walked outside and headed back toward the courthouse and the homeless encampment across the street from it, all but blocking the entrance to Screaming Eagle Bail Bonds. When he arrived, he stepped between two men sleeping on flattened cardboard and slipped into the business to find it once again empty except for Edna, the multilingual office assistant. She was on the phone again, speaking yet another language he didn't recognize.

He waited for her to finish her call, then held up the business card that had been left with Laura. "Is Mr. Yu here? I think he wants to talk with me."

Edna looked up from her computer monitor. She was wearing a cap-sleeve blouse that again showed off the menagerie of black-line tattoos covering most of her arms. Raine noticed the letters E-D-N-A tattooed on the fingers of her left hand as she reached for the phone. "I'll see if he's available.

"Mr. Raine is here to see you," she said into the receiver after a moment.

Raine was initially pleased that she remembered his name. Then he considered they had probably just been talking about him, and not favorably.

"Okay, I'll tell him." Edna hung up the phone and looked

up at him with thickly lined eyes. "Mr. Yu will be out in a few minutes. He's on a call."

Raine wondered how Yu could be on a call while also answering the call from Edna, but he decided not to question it. Instead, he decided to pass the time by questioning Edna.

"So, how are you liking the job?" he asked. "Sebastian said you just started not too long ago."

Edna paused before answering, as if trying to decide whether she wanted to. "I like the job fine, Mr. Raine. It's not very exciting, but we help people."

"That's important," Raine agreed. He glanced back toward the exit and what lay beyond. "I think my friend, Rebecca, is helping you find a new location. That's still on track, right?"

"I believe so," Edna replied. She too looked toward the exit. "That's a very complicated problem. I don't like the idea of just moving away and pretending it doesn't exist."

Raine frowned slightly and nodded. "You're right. It is complicated. But maybe you can move and also try to help. That might offer the excitement you're looking for."

Edna shrugged. "I imagine being a criminal defense attorney can be exciting sometimes."

"Sometimes," Raine agreed. "Sometimes not. And sometimes too exciting."

"Oh, yeah?" Edna invited with a raised eyebrow.

But Raine could hardly tell her about firing his gun in the middle of Magnolia. "I'm afraid I can't share details. Attorney-client privilege. Or attorney work product. Some rule that keeps stuff private."

Edna frowned, an expression lent extra weight by her candy apple red lips.

"Hey, maybe you should look into becoming a paralegal," Raine suggested as a way to assuage any hurt feelings. "Someone with your language skills could really advance quick—"

"Dan!" Sebastian Yu emerged from his office to call out to Raine and interrupt his sales pitch. "Thanks for coming. Step inside my office."

Raine excused himself from Edna and followed Yu into his office.

"You wanted to see me?" Raine began. "Did Rebecca not come through for you? She said she would. I can follow up with her."

"Oh, no, no, no." Yu waved the suggestion away. "Rebecca is the best. In fact, I don't understand how someone like you got an in with someone like her."

"Someone like me?" Raine questioned with a friendly laugh. "People like me are what keep you in business."

"People like your clients," Yu corrected. "Or some of them anyway. I wanted to talk to you about one of them, in fact. One of them who could cost me a great deal of money if he's late for court again."

Raine nodded. At least he knew why he was there. "How did you find out about that? He made it to court. It was just some bad traffic. The judge didn't forfeit your bail."

"But the prosecutor asked him to," Yu replied. "I got a call from a connection of mine in the clerk's office. The bailiff was already preparing the order to forfeit my bail money. That's half a million dollars, Dan. I can't just lose that. I need to get it back at the end of the case. But to get it back, your guy needs to show up for court. A different judge might have forfeited that bail."

Raine knew that was true. He also knew Yu could, at any

time, go to the court, declare that he no longer felt secure, and get his money back. And Hawkins would go back into custody.

"I'll talk to him, Sebastian," Raine assured. "It won't happen again. In fact, he's going to stay in a hotel during the trial to make sure it doesn't happen again."

Yu's eyebrows knitted together. "A hotel? Is he not in the area anymore?"

"What? Ha! No. No, of course he's in the area." Raine didn't define what he meant by 'area'. "He's not going anywhere. I promise. I just wanted you to know that he won't be late again. That little snafu scared him too. The last thing he wants to do is go back into custody."

Yu nodded a few times, then smiled. "Okay. That's good enough for me. For now. But if I hear that he's so much as five minutes late again, I'm taking my money and going home."

"That's fair." Raine raised his hands in agreement. "Absolutely fair."

Problem handled. "So, tell me about the new office search. What does Rebecca have in mind for you?"

It was just a little more massaging. Something for Yu to remember him by, in case any new problems might arise after he left. But Raine knew he could only delay his next task for so long.

There was definitely more massaging in Raine's immediate future.

20

Raine returned to the Peony Spa the day before the readiness hearing. He had largely given up hope of finding a smoking gun sufficient to convince Alexander to dismiss the case, especially on the eve of trial. But he still needed evidence strong enough to convince a jury of law-abiding, middle-class citizens who actually responded to their jury summons that a very bad man might resort to killing his own daughter. Especially if that daughter was about to expose that very bad man's human trafficking operation.

Raine knew it was a bit of a leap from the single assault on a single masseuse he and Sommers had witnessed to a full-blown human trafficking operation, but sometimes leaps were correct. And it wasn't an uneducated leap. Raine had seen a lot in his professional life. He knew the basics of human trafficking. Trick young foreign women to come to the country for a better life, then force them to work in sleazy spas, providing 'happy ending' massages, and more, while Szabo held onto their passports and threatened them with deportation and violence if they so much as thought of calling the cops. Sommers had done some digging, and the same anonymous corporation that owned the Peony Spa owned several more in town. If all of them were involved, it was a large operation indeed. Large enough to kill to protect it.

But Raine needed proof of the operation, or else it would remain nothing more than a theory. A theory that Alexander would ignore and Wooten would suppress from the trial as rank speculation. He could hardly ask Sommers to accompany him, so he was on his own for the reconnaissance mission at the Peony Spa.

He booked a massage at the very end of the day. He wanted the place to be empty of other customers who might overhear and full of masseuses tired enough to slip up and accidentally provide him useful information. He just needed to be sure to leave before anything illegal happened. Gaining useful information against Szabo was all the 'happy ending' he needed.

Raine parked at the far end of the lot and walked slowly to the front door. He was trying to look nonchalant. He didn't know if he was pulling it off, but he thought it was better than rushing inside. He wanted to be like any other customer, typical and forgettable. Anonymous.

The door to the spa opened with a tinkle of bells mounted above the door frame. Inside, Raine was greeted by a sense-pleasing combination of dimmed lights, fragrant incense, and the sound of running water in a wall-mounted fountain.

"Welcome to Peony Spa," the woman behind the counter greeted him. She was middle-aged, with silky black hair and dark lips. "How may we be of service to you today, sir?"

Raine glanced around quickly to ensure no one else was in the lobby, then he stepped up to the front counter. "Um, I'm interested in a massage. A full massage."

"A massage," the receptionist repeated. "Of course, sir."

"A full massage," Raine repeated. He wasn't entirely sure what the latest code words were, but he supposed a nervous first-time customer wouldn't know either.

The woman smiled gracefully. "Of course, sir. Understood, sir. Do you have a particular girl in mind? A referral, perhaps?"

There were message boards where frequent visitors to prostitution fronts would rate and recommend particular workers. Raine hadn't bothered to check them out. He didn't think he really wanted to read what those men had to say.

"Um, no. No one special," Raine answered. Then he added, "Someone with experience, I guess. And a pretty face?"

The woman smiled again. "Of course, sir. Very good, sir. Can I have your first name, please? Your first name only."

"Uh, David," he lied. It was close to his real name, but otherwise common. Forgettable.

"David," the woman repeated with a luscious smile. "Thank you, Mr. David. And how will you be paying, Mr. David, sir?"

"Cash?" Raine inquired. He could hardly use a credit card with a different name at that point.

"Of course, sir." The woman was nonplussed at the idea of cash payment. Another clue that the spa was more than just a spa. "Please have a seat, sir. Jasmine will be out to gather you in just a few minutes."

Raine thanked the woman and found a seat on a green, crushed velvet loveseat next to the fountain. The lobby was

so relaxing that part of him hoped they really did just do
normal massages. Maybe he could just get one of those and
head home refreshed and relaxed ahead of the impending
readiness hearing. But that would leave him empty-handed.
He needed that motive for Emil Szabo to kill his daughter.
He needed evidence. He needed a—

"Massage for Mr. David?" a woman's voice interrupted
his thoughts. "Massage special for Mr. David?"

Raine turned to see a woman he presumed was Jasmine.
She was tall and thin, with black hair that trailed down the
full length of her back. She was wearing a lavender robe,
cinched tightly at her narrow waist, and white kitten heels.
Another clue. A reputable masseuse wasn't going to wear
heels while standing on her feet all day.

"I'm David." Raine raised an index finger and stood up.

"Hello, Mr. David. I'm Jasmine." The woman was holding
open the door to the back of the spa. "Please come this way,
sir."

Raine did as instructed and followed Jasmine through
the door. Once within the business, Raine noted the lights
were even dimmer and the scent of incense was even
stronger. Jasmine led him to a room in the far back of the
spa, passing a dozen other rooms, their doors closed, their
customers undoubtedly enjoying whatever services were
being provided.

"This room, please," Jasmine said. "Take off all your
clothes and lie on the table."

"All of my clothes?" Raine asked, trying not to sound like
a cop.

"Yes, sir."

"And lie face down or face up?"

"Whichever you prefer, Mr. David, sir." Jasmine smiled

broadly, then gestured again for Raine to step inside. He did so, and she closed the door behind him.

The table was covered in fresh sheets, which Raine appreciated. There was no chair to set his clothes on, but there were hooks behind the door. He slowly undressed, wondering at what point did he stop investigating a crime and start committing one. He elected to keep his underwear on, against instructions, and lie face down. Hopefully, he would simply seem nervous about his first time, and not like an undercover cop trying to avoid creating an entrapment defense. After a few minutes, there was a knock on the door, and Jasmine stepped back into the room.

"I, uh, I was cold." Raine gestured toward his underwear. It was definitely not cold in the room, but he felt a need to explain himself. Then he changed the subject. "So, um, have you been doing this long?"

Jasmine didn't answer immediately. She walked to the back of the room, and Raine could hear her pump lotion into her hands. "Not long," she answered.

"Where are you from?" Raine asked. "I mean, like, originally."

Another pause, then, "Malaysia."

"Oh, nice," he felt like he should say. "I've never been to Malaysia."

Jasmine grabbed his shoulders and began what seemed to be a perfectly normal massage.

Raine lowered his head into the circular face rest. "So, you came here from Malaysia not too long ago?"

"Yes," Jasmine answered. "How is the massage? Too much pressure?"

"No, no. The pressure is perfect," Raine answered before getting back to his own questions. "What, uh, what made you come to the United States? Was it work? Like a job waiting for you?"

Jasmine stopped rubbing his back. "Oh, I forgot my lotion. I'll be right back."

"But you have lotion," Raine protested, lifting his head out of its cushioned cradle.

"No, no. Special lotion." She pushed his head back down into the face rest. "You want the special lotion, I know. Wait here. I'll be right back."

Raine heard her exit and the door close behind her. He kept his face in the cushion. So far, so good, he told himself. Jasmine seemed to fit the profile of a woman being trafficked for prostitution. He just needed to get the information out of her before she made him roll over and tried to finish their transaction.

He didn't hear the door open again. Whoever came into the room must have done so when she stepped out. He saw the briefest glimpse of a man's shoe below his face before he felt the crushing blow to the back of his head and blacked out.

21

The throbbing in the front of his skull was almost as bad as the sharp pain to the back of it. Or maybe it was the other way around. Either way, Raine's head was killing him as he forced his eyes open and tried to remember where he was or what he was doing. The rope on his wrists accelerated his recall.

"Shit," he hissed under his breath.

The details of the room were hard to make out. At first, because his vision was blurry, but as things came into focus, he had to squint against the darkness to make out a metal shelving unit of cleaning supplies and the outline of a door with light on the other side of it. He was in some sort of supply closet. He was seated on a surprisingly comfortable chair, given the circumstances, metal with vinyl cushions. The comfort was limited, however, by the strain on his arms from having them tied to the back of the chair. He thought he felt dried blood on the back of his neck as well. He deduced he was still at the spa, but he had no idea how long he had been unconscious. He was still wearing just his underwear, but noticed the rest of his clothes balled up in the corner by the door. They must have cleaned the room out for the next customer while they decided what to do with him. They were still running a business after all. Raine could admire the hustle.

The door opened then, with a groan of its hinges, and Raine squinted against the light that spilled into the storage room. The silhouette of a large man filled the doorway.

"Oh, good. You're awake," the man said in a voice Raine recalled hearing before.

The man stepped into the room and flicked on the overhead light.

Raine instinctively shut his eyes against the light but forced them open as fast as he could muster. He wanted to see what was coming. And who would be delivering it. If he had thought he might be confronted by Emil Szabo himself, he wasn't far off. The scar over what had been the man's left eye was a dead giveaway.

"Alexei Szabo," Raine said. "I should have shot you at Hawkins's house."

"That was you?" Alexei grinned. "Oh, good. Now I can pay you back for that, too."

Then he punched Raine full-force in the mouth.

Raine waited for the wave of pain to subside, then spat a mouthful of blood on the floor.

"You're defending the man who murdered my sister," Alexei said.

"Gotta pay the bills, right?" Raine shrugged as well as he could with his arms tied behind his back. "So you guys own this place? That's a crazy coincidence."

"You coming here doesn't seem like a coincidence," Alexei said. "It seems like harassment."

"Well, hitting me over the head and tying me to a chair seems like assault," Raine replied. "So, why don't we call it even and you let me go? I'll even pay for the massage."

"Seems like assault, huh?" Alexei laughed. Then he stepped forward and punched Raine in the mouth again. "Does that seem like assault?"

Raine turned his head and spat more blood onto the floor. "Yeah, that's definitely assault."

"Why did you come here?" Alexei demanded.

"To get a massage," Raine answered. "Obviously."

Alexei glared down at him. "You were asking a lot of questions for someone who just wanted a massage."

"I'm a lawyer," Raine defended. "That's what I do."

Another punch, that time to his left eye. Raine saw stars and felt a sharp pain in his brow. Blood began to ooze down his face from a cut above his eye. He tried not to give Alexei the satisfaction of showing his pain, but the blows hurt. He might not have had both eyes, but he had large hands and strong arms.

"Let me ask another question," Raine tried. Conversation was better than a beating. "What's the end game here? Are you really going to murder me? Because that's a really big deal, and I'd have to be an idiot to come here without telling people where I was going. I may be a lot of things, but I'm not an idiot."

He had, however, completely failed to tell anyone where he was going.

"If I go missing," Raine continued, "the first place the cops are going to look is here. Now, aside from the fact that I bet you and your dad do not want the cops sniffing around this particular business, do you have any idea how hard it is to cover up a murder? I've already spat my DNA all over the floor, and more of it is dripping off my face right now. Most methods of killing people involve spilling even more DNA. Murder is messy, and it's basically impossible to get rid of every last cell of DNA left behind by the victim. You think your father is going to go down on a murder charge? I mean, I'm sure he's a great father. He obviously inspires a dangerous level of loyalty, but he's still a businessman first. You get caught, suddenly he doesn't know you. You know what I mean? And then you're the one who spends thirty years in Walla Walla for a murder you didn't even have your own motive to commit."

Alexei didn't respond, but he also didn't punch Raine again.

"But look, my offer still stands," Raine continued. "You say I harassed you. You have definitely assaulted me. Let's call that good. I don't like cops either, so if you let me go, I'm not reporting any of this. It's over, and we both get back to our day jobs. What do you say?"

Alexei stared down menacingly, his frown growing deeper. Finally, he took a half-step back and kicked Raine in the center of his chest, sending him flying backward and landing on his side, his right arm pinned painfully under the back of the chair it was tied to.

"Wait here." Alexei laughed. Then he left again, closing the door behind him but leaving the light on.

Raine struggled to get up again, if for no other reason than to prevent the circulation to his arm from being cut off. He couldn't manage to get back into an upright position, but he was able to pull his arm down to where the back of the chair narrowed, where it connected to the seat. There was enough space to let the blood flow, and his fingers tingled at the return of it. Outside, he could hear the muffled half of a telephone conversation.

"He says he told someone he came here tonight... I don't know. He didn't say... Oh yeah, I can definitely get him to tell me."

Raine didn't like the sound of that.

"Yeah, we got tons of bleach."

He didn't like the sound of that either. Bleach was the one thing that actually did destroy DNA.

"Like a plastic tarp? I mean, I might have something like that in my truck."

Raine really didn't like the sound of that. He started pulling at the ropes around his wrists to see if he might be able to wriggle free. It was no use. The rope was tight. He wasn't going to be able to just pull his arms free.

"I don't think you want to wrap the body in plastic," Alexei was saying, far too within earshot for Raine's comfort. "That makes it mummify. You want it to decompose into the dirt."

Raine began struggling against the ropes, despite knowing it was no use. He needed to get free before he ended up in a shallow grave with no one knowing where he was when he disappeared.

"Yeah, yeah. I'll check my truck... No, he's not going anywhere. I left him on the floor tied to a chair... Yeah, I know, hilarious, right?"

Then, "I'll call you back when it's done," and the sound of the man's footsteps retreating, presumably to his truck.

"Shit, shit, shit, shit." Raine was trying not to panic, but he felt like he had good reason to. With all of his strength, he managed to push himself off the floor and get back into an upright position. But his hands were still bound to the chair behind him, so he could only fall back into the same help-less sitting position.

"Think, Raine, think," he told himself. "There has to be a solution."

He considered trying to dislocate or maybe even break his own thumb to be able to pull one hand free. But his hands couldn't grasp each other the way they were tied. He couldn't have broken his thumb if he'd wanted to—which he didn't really, but it would have been preferable to what was going to happen when Alexei returned.

The metal chair couldn't be broken into splinters by smashing it onto the floor. Maybe he could hide behind the door and launch a surprise attack when the man returned. Kicks and headbutts and swinging chair legs and... that would never work.

Raine hung his head. "I'm dead."

A few moments later, the door groaned again, and Raine looked up to see whether Alexei had a gun or a knife in his hand. The smart play was a plastic bag to suffocate him—less DNA—but that sounded like the worst way to go.

Instead, Raine was stunned to see the woman from the front desk. "You!"

"Shh!" the woman scolded. "Be silent."

She had a knife in her hand, but instead of plunging it into his neck or something similar, she hurried around behind him and started sawing at the rope.

"Pull your arms apart," she whispered. "As hard as you can. It can't look like a clean cut."

Raine wasn't about to argue. He pulled his wrists apart as the woman continued sawing at the rope. After a few seconds, the rope snapped and unfurled from his wrists. He was free.

He sprang to his feet, rubbing his wrists. "Thank you."

"Shut up," the woman hissed, even as she laid the chair back down on the floor. "Turn left and run to the end of the hallway. There's an emergency exit. Hurry!"

Raine didn't have to be told twice. He threw the broken rope on the floor, snagged his pants from the pile by the door, and bolted for the exit.

Behind him, he heard the woman step into the hallway and shout in the opposite direction. "He got away! The ropes snapped when you kicked him over, you idiot! He's gone!"

No alarm went off when Raine slammed through the emergency exit. It was fully dark outside, although he had no idea if it was midnight or 4:00 a.m. It didn't matter. He ran straight for the lights of Michigan Street, then south to the nearest business. Something had to be open somewhere. An all-night diner or a bar that hadn't reached closing time yet. Anywhere with people, witnesses.

Sure enough, there was a twenty-four seven grocery store on the corner of the next block. Raine ran inside and kept going to the back of the store, where he doubled over to catch his breath. He was reasonably sure he was safe again. And he was absolutely sure he was going to bill Hawkins double for however many hours he'd just spent at the Assault and Battery Spa.

22

"What the hell happened to you?" Hawkins's jaw dropped when Raine walked into Judge Wooten's courtroom later that morning.

"Werewolves," Raine replied. "Always say werewolves. It's mysterious and usually ends further inquiry."

"I'll go ahead and inquire further," Hawkins said. "What happened?"

They were in one of the eight identical courtrooms on the sixth floor of the King County Courthouse. It was still fourteen minutes before the 9:00 a.m. scheduled time of the readiness hearing. It was little more than a formality. And a bit of a showcase. Hawkins was the only one in the room when Raine entered. Alexander would arrive soon enough, followed by the bailiff and court reporter, then finally the judge himself. They didn't have a lot of time for small talk.

Raine had a fat lip surrounded by a purple bruise, plus a black eye with a cut over it held together by a butterfly bandage. He looked like he had won a prize fight. "You should see the other guy." He knew he could have been a lot worse. Six feet under worse.

"Seriously, Dan." Hawkins put a hand on Raine's shoulder. "What happened?"

Raine sighed. He appreciated the weight of his friend's hand, but he couldn't forget the friend was why he was injured in the first place. "Night before trial. My place. I'll supply the bourbon. And I'll tell you everything."

Hawkins smiled. "Agreed."

"But," Raine added, "you tell me everything, too. We're about to go to battle, my friend. There are no secrets in a foxhole."

Hawkins nodded. "That's not the saying. But you've got it, friend."

Alexander arrived then. He carried the same aura of humble invulnerability he always did. Raine wouldn't begrudge him a reputation as a skilled and effective trial attorney, but he held onto the comfort that it was easier to win all of your cases when you were a prosecutor. Most defendants were guilty, and the cops did all the work for you. To some extent, you just needed to show up and look good in a suit. Alexander definitely wasn't risking his life in the back rooms of seedy spas.

The prosecutor reached the front of the court and got his first good look at Raine's battered face. "Are you all right, Mr. Raine?"

Raine appreciated the concern. It seemed genuine. That didn't mean he couldn't have fun with it. "Yeah. Why?"

Alexander took a beat. "Um, no reason. So, uh, are we ready for trial on Monday? No reason to delay the proceedings?"

"None from the defense," Raine answered with a slight

lisp from his swollen lip. He turned to his client. "Right, Judge?"

"Right," Hawkins answered. "Let's get this over with."

Alexander smiled tightly and nodded. "Very well then. This should be quick."

And quick it was. At exactly 9:00 a.m., the bailiff called out his exhortation to "All rise!" and announced the entrance of The Honorable Visiting Judge Frank Wooten.

Wooten bade the litigants to be seated and asked the only question that mattered that morning. "Are the parties ready to proceed to trial on Monday?" he asked. "Mr. Alexander?"

Alexander stood to address the Court. "The State is ready, Your Honor."

Wooten nodded and turned to the defense table, taking a moment for the first time to really look at the defense attorney. "Mr. Raine, is the def— Mr. Raine? Are you quite all right?"

Raine smiled as best he could through the bruises. "Yes, Your Honor. I'm perfectly fine. And the defense is ready for trial on Monday. Thank you."

Wooten hesitated as he scanned Raine's injuries further. Finally, he stammered, "Uh, okay, well, good then. Trial will commence promptly at nine a.m. on Monday morning. Are there any other issues which need the Court's attention this morning?"

Raine looked to Alexander and shrugged.

Alexander turned his face only slightly to Raine, before directing his comments to the bench. "Nothing from the State, Your Honor."

"Anything from the defense?" Wooten inquired.

Raine looked to Hawkins, who shook his head in reply.

Raine looked back to the judge. "Nothing from the defense, Your Honor. We look forward to our day in court."

Judge Wooten laughed. "It's going to be a lot more than one day, Mr. Raine. But yes, it will be good to get this case tried. A lot of people are waiting on this result."

The comment made Raine realize there were again no cameras in the courtroom. But he knew they would be there on Monday.

"If there is nothing else then," Wooten raised his gavel, "court is adjourned until Monday morning at nine o'clock. Enjoy your weekends, if you can."

The gavel came down with a bang, and the hearing was concluded. Wooten retreated to his chambers, and Alexander exited almost as quickly. The bailiff and court reporter were close behind. Raine and Hawkins were left alone in the courtroom.

"See you Sunday?" Hawkins asked. "Eight p.m.?"

"Eight sounds perfect," Raine answered. "It'll be like old times."

"Not quite," Hawkins replied. "We never had a case where one of us was the defendant."

Raine couldn't argue with that. "Let's keep it to just this one. I don't need that kind of trouble."

Hawkins pointed at his friend's face. "Looks like you found a different kind of trouble."

"Different," Raine allowed, "but related."

He shook his friend's hand. "See you Sunday."

23

Raine had one more thing he needed to take care of before trial started. He didn't really want to do it, but sticking his head in the sand wouldn't change the reality of the situation. The bruises on his face spurred him to action.

He knocked on the door of the home he had once shared with his now ex-wife Natalie and stepped back to wait for her to open the door.

"Dan? What are you doing here?" she asked before she got a good look at him. "You don't pick up the boys again until—" She finally saw his face. "Oh my God! What happened to you?"

"Werewolves," Raine joked.

Natalie didn't laugh.

"Okay, the details aren't important, but I've gotten a little too deep in one of my cases. There are some seriously bad guys on the other side."

"They did this to you?" Natalie asked. She started to reach out to touch his bruised face, but Raine recoiled, for several reasons.

"One of them did," Raine answered. "But to be fair, my hands were tied behind my back. I could have taken him in a fair fight. Although I guess he only has one eye, so..."

"What the hell are you talking about?" Natalie's voice elevated in both volume and pitch. "Are you in danger?"

Raine shrugged slightly. "I mean, yes. I guess. I got away, but that doesn't mean they won't try again. And I'm worried they might try to get at me through you and the boys."

"Is this what you were trying to tell me about when I dropped the boys off?" Natalie's eyes flew wide. "What did you get us involved in, Dan?"

"I don't think you're actually in danger, Nat," Raine tried to reassure her. "But it's not a zero possibility either. So, I don't know, maybe you could take my weekend with the boys and go on a trip or something? Oregon coast? Olympic Peninsula? Disneyland? I can buy the park tickets."

Natalie ran her hands through her thick brown hair. "Oh my God," she said again, but with a different tone. "I thought I was done having to worry about you and your job. That's what a divorce means, right? I don't have to worry about you screwing up my life. Why is it still happening?"

"We have kids in common," Raine answered. "I'll be messing up their lives and yours until the day I die. Although that might be sooner rather than later."

Natalie dropped her shoulders. "Is that supposed to be funny?"

"I don't know," Raine answered, "but it's true."

Natalie raised a hand to her face and shook her head. "Really? The Oregon Coast? For how long? Is this another one of your months-long cases?"

"Yeah," he confirmed, "but I think things will be safer

once the trial starts next week. I don't think they'll make a move after that. The next few days are the most dangerous."

Natalie shook her head, but her expression softened ever so slightly when she looked at his battered face again. "You need to heal up before the trial. Juries don't trust lawyers who lose fights to werewolves."

"Who said I lost?" Raine quipped. Then, in a serious tone again, "We start up on Monday. Let me know if you want me to buy those Disneyland tickets."

"They're a little too old for Disneyland," Natalie replied. "We'll think of something else."

"Okay," Raine answered. "Thanks for listening to me."

Natalie laughed and looked to the sky. "I don't know whether to thank you for the warning or punch you for making it necessary in the first place. You deserve both."

"I know." Raine nodded with a bittersweet smile. "That's why we got divorced."

24

Raine usually spent the night before trial alone. It was a time to reflect and recharge, to contemplate and consider, to conclude and prepare. But that night, it was also a time to commune and converse, to reconnect and recharge. As promised, Raine supplied the bourbon. Ten-year-old, oak-barrel aged. Raine poured them each a shot, neat, and they settled in on his balcony, with its mostly obstructed view of downtown Seattle.

"We've had the privilege to live long, interesting lives, seeing the worst things men do to their fellow men," Hawkins observed.

"It does make you question," Raine replied, "whether there's a greater good to even aspire to."

"Agreed," Hawkins said. He raised his glass. "The only evidence I've found for the existence of God is the existence of bourbon. Here's to old friends and new victories."

"Old friends." Raine tapped his glass against Hawkins's and took a sip of the sweet brown liquid. "I'll drink to victories after they're secured."

Hawkins nodded. "Fair enough." Then, after a moment, "So, are you going to tell me what happened to you?"

Raine took a deep breath, then a deeper drink of his bourbon, and told the story. The stakeout with Sommers, Sokolowski, Jasmine, too many questions, the blow to his head, the rope and the chair, the punches, and the plastic tarp in the truck. And the mystery woman who saved his life.

"Holy shit," Hawkins gasped. "You're lucky to be alive."

Raine took another sip of bourbon. "I am. So you owe it to me to tell the truth. Do you think Trevor did it?"

Hawkins sighed and looked down into his own drink. "Well, I didn't murder Lydia. That means someone else did. Was it Emil Szabo? God, I hope so. But if it wasn't him, then I know the next best suspect is Trevor. It's always the boyfriend, right?"

"Right," Raine confirmed. "He could have shot her, then hid and waited to blend in with everyone else when they ran into the room. The jury would believe that."

Hawkins frowned. "He's my son. My only child. I had such expectations for him when he was born. He was going to be a baseball star, and a straight-A student, and date every girl from kindergarten to senior year. Everything I never was."

"We all think that when our first kid is born," Raine commiserated. "And then we watch them throw a ball for the first time and realize the reality might be different."

Hawkins laughed. "Don't get me wrong. I love him. But sometimes, I just don't get it. Why would he move home after college? Why didn't he move into some crappy studio bachelor's pad where he could take drugs and hook up with girls like a normal twenty-year-old? And how did he possibly land a woman like Lydia Szabo?"

"They were arguing that night," Raine said. "Did he know you kept that gun in your desk?"

"I'm sure he did," Hawkins admitted. "I don't remember ever specifically telling him, but it wasn't a secret."

"It's not too late to change tack," Raine suggested. "After what Szabo's son did to me, I can blame at least three people now. Trevor would just be one suspect of many."

But Hawkins shook his head. "No. I'm not getting out of this by throwing my own son under the bus."

"Admirable," Raine replied with another sip of bourbon. "Stupid, but admirable."

Hawkins looked at Raine. "Would you throw one of your boys under the bus to avoid taking a punishment for them, even one you didn't deserve?"

Raine thought for a moment. "For Jordan, maybe. For Jason, probably not. He's been a jerk to me since the divorce."

Hawkins laughed. "You'd do it for either of them, and you know it."

They sat in silence for several comfortable minutes. Silence between friends was warm. Raine was reminded of what he had lost when Hawkins left their partnership to be a judge. But he was also aware that he could never get that back. That just wasn't how life worked.

Finally, Hawkins broke the silence. "Dan?"

"Yeah?"

"Can we win?"

Raine took a deep breath, then finished the last of his bourbon. "Can we? Absolutely. Will we? I don't know. But I promise you, Mike, I'll do my best."

25

Nine o'clock Monday morning saw Visiting Judge Wooten's borrowed courtroom filled to the brim. Cameras and reporters filled the last row of the gallery. The remainder of the seats were taken up by interested members of the public and curious members of the local bar. At the front of the courtroom were the counsel tables. Alexander sat alone at the prosecution table. Raine and Hawkins sat together at the defense table. The bailiff and court reporter took up the seats directly below the bench. And then Judge Wooten entered the courtroom.

"All rise! The King County Superior Court is now in session, The Honorable Frank Wooten, visiting judge, presiding."

"Are the parties ready to proceed," he asked as he sat down and everyone else followed his lead, "on the matter of *The State of Washington versus Michael Hawkins*?"

Alexander stood to address the Court first. "The State is ready, Your Honor."

Raine stood next. "The defense is ready as well, Your Honor."

And they were off.

But before the trial could begin in earnest, before the action the cameras and spectators had come to see would take place, before the battle was truly joined, there were preliminary matters to attend to. Chief among these were scheduling and selecting a jury. Working out the daily schedule, and exceptions thereto, could take hours. Selecting a jury would take days. The cameras would stop coming until the jury was picked and it was time for opening statements. The spectators would fluctuate depending on whether they were members of the public or members of the bar, and whether they were interested in learning a thing or two about what happened behind the scenes of the criminal justice system.

Judge Wooten ordered a pool of one hundred potential jurors. From those hundred, twelve jurors and two alternates would be selected. The remaining eighty-six of the potential jurors would be questioned but ultimately excused for one reason or another. Alexander and Raine took turns ostensibly asking the jurors questions about their qualifications to sit on the case, but really using the questioning process to begin shaping opinions about the evidence to come. The judge also interjected to pose a fair number of his own questions.

At the end of the questioning, the lawyers didn't actually get to select the people who would sit on the jury—not directly. Instead, each side got to strike eight potential jurors they didn't like, six for the main panel and two more for each alternate. At the end, after the jurors who were obviously pro-prosecution were stricken by Raine, the ones who seemed sympathetic to the defense were stricken by Alexander, and the ones for whom sitting on a weeks-long murder trial would result in a loss of job or other hardship were released by Judge Wooten, the first twelve jurors left standing would be the jury, the next two the alternates. The jurors weren't the people either side wanted. They were the ones left over after the desirable people were eliminated. The best way to get picked for a jury was to get a seat in the front row and keep your mouth shut.

The following Monday, Judge Wooten reconvened the trial, the jury was empaneled, and the cameras were back in the courtroom. Alexander, Raine, and Hawkins were seated and ready. It was finally go time.

"Good luck, boys." Cindy Hawkins gave her husband one last hug before the trial started and she had to leave the courtroom. "I wish I could stay."

"You're a witness," Hawkins answered. "Witnesses stay in the hall until they testify."

She nodded, bravely even, but her lip quivered. She turned to Raine and pointed her index finger at him. "You protect my husband. Do you hear me? You win this case, Daniel Raine. I'm counting on you."

"I'll do my best," was all Raine could offer. But he meant it.

Cindy departed then, and soon thereafter, the judge and jury entered.

"Ladies and gentlemen of the jury," Judge Wooten began the proceedings, "please give your attention to Mr. Alexander, who will deliver the opening statement on behalf of the plaintiff, the State of Washington."

26

All eyes turned to Alexander. He stood up calmly, buttoned his suit coat, and stepped out from behind the prosecutor's counsel table. "May it please the Court," he began formally, with a nod to each named entity in turn, "counsel, members of the jury."

Then he took up a position directly in front of the jury box, centered and close enough to signal confidence, but not too close as to be aggressive. Then, with every person in the room hanging on his next word, he began.

"The smoking gun," he said. "That phrase has come to mean absolute, incontrovertible evidence. We use it in every field, every discipline, every arena of our lives, when we want to convey that we have uncovered evidence beyond certainty that a particular proposition is, in fact, true. And in this case, the defendant was literally found holding the smoking gun. He was holding that smoking gun, seen by a dozen witnesses, as he stood over the woman he had just murdered, Lydia Szabo, his son's girlfriend."

Raine appreciated Alexander's coopting the smoking

gun metaphor for his opening. It was almost too literal, Raine thought, but that's what made it impossible to pass up.

"Now the defendant, Michael Hawkins, sits in this courtroom, accused of murder, and despite the fact that he was found holding the literal smoking gun, he is presumed innocent. He has the right to a trial. But being presumed innocent isn't the same thing as being innocent. And having the right to a trial doesn't mean you won't be found guilty at the end of it. In fact, in this trial, the State will put on more than sufficient evidence to convince each and every one of you that the defendant is guilty of the murder of Lydia Szabo."

Alexander delivered his words with a cool confidence that was consistent with his reputation as one of, if not the, top homicide prosecutors in the county. He didn't seem cocky, just in command of the case. He knew the facts backward and forward, and he would deliver them to the jury. But, Raine knew, every strength held its own vulnerability.

"In order to prove the charge of murder beyond a reasonable doubt, the State will be calling a long list of witnesses. Not one of these witnesses can tell you the entire story. Each will bring you a part of the story, and it will be our job, yours and mine together, to piece that story together into the coherent whole that will lead to a verdict of guilty."

Maybe a little cocky, Raine thought of his opponent. He glanced over at his client, but Hawkins didn't return the look; he was staring directly at Alexander, eyes boring through the back of his perfectly tailored suit coat.

"The first witness you will hear from is Lydia Szabo's father," Alexander continued. "One of the elements of murder is that the victim was a living, breathing human being. That, unfortunately, is a fact that can be lost in the bloodless formality of a criminal trial. So, before we get into what the defendant did to her, and why, you deserve to know a little more about her."

Alexander took a moment to allow the jury to lean forward a bit in their seats. He took a half-step to his right and shifted his weight into a slightly more familiar stance. "Lydia Szabo was a twenty-year-old aspiring interior decorator. Her family own several small businesses across the city. Small mom-and-pop operations like a dry cleaner's downtown and an ice cream stand near Green Lake."

And an international human trafficking ring, Raine wanted to add. But he knew he would get his chance.

"One day, not too long before her untimely demise," Alexander went on, "Lydia ran into a handsome young man at a coffee shop. They struck up a conversation and found each other interesting enough to schedule a dinner date. That date led to more dates, and soon they were what people in my generation would call boyfriend-girlfriend. That young man was Trevor Hawkins, the defendant's son. And that chance encounter in the coffee shop was the first step toward Lydia being murdered in her boyfriend's home." He paused. "But I'm getting ahead of myself."

Alexander was very much not getting ahead of himself, Raine knew. The exact length and cadence of the opening was intentional, premeditated even. But Alexander was delivering it so smoothly that it felt like he was telling the story for the first time—because the truth didn't need to be rehearsed.

"Trevor had recently graduated from college," Alexander continued, "and, like so many of his generation, he was trying to get on his feet so he could spread his wings and leave the nest. He had moved back home with his parents and taken up residence in the family's detached pool house."

Raine frowned slightly. Jurors were regular people, and most regular people didn't have pool houses. Regular people also were often jealous of people who had pool houses. They would relish a chance to stick it to someone of a higher station in life. Someone like Hawkins.

"It wasn't an ideal situation," Alexander explained, "but it was good enough. Or so it seemed to Trevor and his mother, Cindy Hawkins, both of whom will be testifying in this trial, even if they might rather not have to do so."

Raine stole another glance at his client. Those eyes staring through Alexander's back narrowed at the mention of his family. Raine suspected any jurors who stole a glance at Hawkins in that moment would interpret his expression as one of displeasure at his family being pushed around by the prosecutor. That was fine with Raine.

"They will tell you," Alexander continued, "that having Trevor at home was uncomfortable, stressful even. The reason was that his father, the defendant, didn't approve of it. And he didn't approve of Lydia Szabo."

A murmur rippled through the jury box, one of curiosity and interest. Everyone loved someone else's family drama.

"To understand why," Alexander undid that half-step, shifting himself back into a formal posture, "I need to tell you a little bit more about the defendant, and about the Szabo family and their businesses."

Alexander turned his upper body just enough to gesture back at Hawkins. "The defendant is no stranger to the courtrooms of the King County Courthouse. It's just that he usually is seated higher. You see, Michael Hawkins is a judge, a judge of this very court. He is still in his first term after being duly elected. He had most recently been serving a tour in the civil department of the court. He presided over non-criminal cases like wrongful death lawsuits, will contests, and," a dramatic pause, "code enforcement actions brought against small businesses. Enterprises like Szabo Enterprises, LLC, the company owned and operated by Lydia's father. And the company whose court case was assigned to Judge Hawkins."

Alexander looked back at Hawkins again and frowned before turning back to the jurors. "Judge Hawkins probably should have recused himself and had the case assigned to a different judge. If he had, perhaps Lydia Szabo would still be alive today. But he didn't, and she isn't. Instead, Judge Hawkins kept the case and decided that he didn't like how Lydia's father conducted business in his city. And he decided he didn't want someone from that family involved with his son."

"That is completely untrue," Hawkins complained to Raine in a whisper. "I never wanted that case. That's why I hired you in the first place."

Raine knew all that, of course. Alexander didn't care.

"There were arguments, recriminations, hurt feelings, and hurt pride," the prosecutor asserted. "You will hear all about that from Trevor and his mother, Cindy. While the defendant never specifically forbade Lydia from coming to the house, she was anything but welcome. Her family had crossed the defendant, and he blamed her for it. And then the defendant decided to throw a fundraiser, well before the next election, because he was so afraid of losing his position as the Honorable Michael Hawkins, Judge of the King County Superior Court. Lydia wasn't really welcome. Trevor brought her anyway."

Raine had to hand it to Alexander. It was a coherent and compelling narrative. If Raine hadn't known all the actual backstory, he might have been persuaded by it as well.

"The fundraiser was a large affair, but it was held at the Hawkinses' home in Magnolia."

The mention of that exclusive neighborhood was another subtle reminder to the regular folks on the jury that Hawkins was rich, and therefore probably thought he was better than them. They'd show him.

"They hired valet parking and catered food from a French restaurant," Alexander piled on the richer-than-thou details. "They even hired some off-duty Seattle police officers to work security, presumably to keep out uninvited guests—like Lydia Szabo.

"You will hear from many of the guests that night," Alexander went on, "as well as the vendors who worked the fundraiser. They will tell you that both the defendant and his wife appeared very anxious, even stressed, trying to control every last detail of the evening. It was a large and important event after all. Everything needed to be perfect. The defendant wanted nothing out of place. But Lydia was there, and she was very much out of place. The defendant wanted her any place but inside his home."

Alexander paused again and shifted his weight to the other side. He sighed, as if personally pained by what he was about to relate. "Eventually, the defendant decided to confront Lydia. By then, his frustration level was at its upper limit. Friends and donors were noticing this young woman who shouldn't be there, not when her family's business had a case in front of the judge. People would talk. Checkbooks would close. Elections, perhaps, would be lost.

"The defendant took Lydia upstairs to his study, away from the crowd. Someplace he could tell her forcefully and in no uncertain terms that she was not welcome in his home, and indeed she was not welcome in his family."

Now he's just guessing, Raine thought. He has no evidence of that. Hawkins certainly didn't tell the police anything like that, and Lydia would just as certainly not be testifying about the substance of a conversation they had, if any.

Alexander shook his head slightly. "The thing about murder cases," he told the jury, telegraphing his experience, and therefore expertise and trustworthiness, "is that no motive ever seems good enough after the fact. No matter what reason one person has for murdering another person, it always seems so small afterward. Everything can and should be sorted out far short of murder. That seems obvious later, but in the heat of the moment, when emotions are high and decisions are rash, that's when murder happens. That's what happened here. The defendant, losing whatever control he'd managed to maintain after an evening of more stress than he could handle, pulled out the loaded semi-automatic pistol he kept in his desk drawer. He pointed it directly at Lydia Szabo's forehead, and he pulled the trigger. Lydia Szabo died instantly and collapsed to the ground. Within seconds, a dozen partygoers, including the defendant's own wife and son, rushed into the room and found the defendant standing over Lydia's dead body."

A dramatic pause.

"The smoking gun in his hand."

Alexander clasped his hands in front of him, a gesture of sincerity, as he ended his opening statement.

"And so, ladies and gentlemen of the jury, based on all of that and more," he said, "I will stand before you again at the end of this trial and ask you to return a verdict of guilty to the crime of murder in the first degree. Thank you."

Alexander turned and walked back to his seat at the prosecution table.

"Thank you, Mr. Alexander," Judge Wooten said before again addressing the jurors. "Now, ladies and gentlemen, please give your attention to Mr. Raine, who will deliver the opening statement on behalf of the defendant."

Raine stood up, patted Hawkins on the back in an intentional gesture of support, and buttoned his suit coat. He stepped out from behind the defense table and walked across the well of the courtroom to the jury box. He didn't bother with a formal, 'May it please the Court...' introduction. No one wanted to hear him say that. The prosecutor had just delivered a compelling, cohesive, coherent argument as to why the defendant was guilty of murder. The jurors wanted to know if Raine had a comeback.

He did, of course. Raine knew he needed to tell the jury that someone else murdered Lydia Szabo. He just didn't know whether he'd be able to prove it. And he still wasn't entirely sure who did it. He knew he wanted it to be Emil Szabo. He also knew it might be Trevor Hawkins. And despite his client's very clear instructions, unexpected things happened in trials. Raine needed to leave himself room to pivot, in case the evidence went a different direction than he expected.

So, he decided not to commit to either Szabo or Trevor in his opening. Instead, he would start throwing grenades and overwhelm everyone with the true facts of the case, leaving the jury dying to know where the evidence would really lead.

"Truth," Raine began, "is stranger than fiction, they say." He pointed back at Alexander. "And that story Mr.

Alexander just told you is most definitely fiction. So, let me tell you the far stranger truth."

One of the problems with always going second was that by the time you took your turn, minds were already half made up. The prosecutor had the advantage of a blank slate. The defense attorney had to try to erase what was written on it. Or you could give the jurors an additional slate and tell an even better story.

"Judge Hawkins was being blackmailed by the Szabo family, who threatened to hurt, maybe even kill his son, Trevor, if Judge Hawkins didn't rule in their favor in that case of theirs. A case he only kept in order to protect his family and insure justice was done."

The courtroom fairly exploded from the allegations in Raine's single first sentence. The packed gallery filled with gasps, the jurors' eyes flew wide, and the heretofore calm and collected prosecutor John Alexander jumped to his feet. "Objection!"

For his part, Judge Wooten was smiling, and not even trying to conceal it. Lawyers in King County often described Pierce County as The Wild West. Alexander's polished opening probably put Wooten half to sleep. But now, he had a gunfight below him.

"Overruled," Wooten declared without bothering to hear the basis of the objection. "This is opening statement. Each lawyer is entitled to tell the jury what they expect the evidence will show. If Mr. Raine fails to deliver on his allegations, I expect the jury will act accordingly."

That was the risk, Raine knew.

Judge Wooten pointed down at Raine. "You may continue, counselor."

"Thank you, Your Honor," Raine replied. He turned again to the jurors, all of whom seemed suddenly very interested in what he had to say. "Judge Hawkins's son, Trevor, owed a large sum of money to the Szabo family. The Szabos don't just run ice cream stands and orphanages or whatever Mr. Alexander said. They also deal in loan-sharking and worse. And all of that was going to come out if that little code enforcement case went too far."

Raine glanced performatively at his opponent, then looked back to the jurors. "Now, what could be worse than loan-sharking and blackmail, you might ask. How about human trafficking? How about owning a collection of spas throughout the city that are a front for trafficking young women from overseas and forcing them into the sex trade?"

"Objection!" Alexander jumped to his feet again. He might as well have shouted, 'Ouch!' Raine was hurting him.

"Overruled," Judge Wooten repeated through a broad, toothy grin.

"That's what Judge Hawkins was fighting against," Raine gestured to his client, "and that's why Lydia became a target. Judge Hawkins had no reason to want Lydia Szabo dead. But her conflicting loyalties between her boyfriend on the one hand and her family on the other led her to be an object of suspicion and fear on all sides. The question isn't, who wanted Lydia Szabo silenced? The question is, why didn't the police look into more than one suspect?"

Another gesture toward the prosecution table. "But actually, we know the answer to that question," Raine continued. "Mr. Alexander just told you the answer. He told you why he's not interested in uncovering the real truth. It was the first three words he spoke to you. 'The smoking gun.' End of story and case closed. It was enough for the cops, it was enough for him, and he wants it to be enough for you."

Raine shook his head like a disappointed schoolteacher. "But you know what, ladies and gentlemen? It is not enough. Not one of the witnesses the State will call to testify will tell you that they saw Michael Hawkins pull the trigger of that gun. Not one. They will only say they saw him holding it, after the murder. And I will promise you right now that despite his constitutional right to remain silent, Judge Hawkins will take the stand and explain that he was the first person to run into the room after the gunshot—the first one to run into unknown danger—and when he saw the gun on the floor he instinctively picked it up to make sure the real killer, whoever that might be, didn't grab it again and hurt more people. And it was only then that all of these smoking gun witnesses rushed into the study. Every one of them will say Judge Hawkins was holding the gun, but not one of them will say he pulled the trigger."

Raine spread his arms wide. "So, who did pull the trigger? Who murdered Lydia Szabo? Well, who doesn't love a good murder mystery? Was it her father, betrayed by her choosing her boyfriend over family? Was it her brother, angry that she had always been the favorite despite his greater loyalty to their clan? Or was it someone else entirely, perhaps a long-lost ex-boyfriend who couldn't let a beautiful young woman go? Or maybe it was something completely unrelated to the difficulties between the Szabo and Hawkins families. Perhaps it was a random party guest or worker, snooping around for something valuable to steal from the affluent hosts, only to be stumbled upon by Lydia and desperate to hide their tracks. We don't know. We don't know because the police had their smoking gun and didn't bother to investigate beyond that. They forgot that it doesn't matter who was holding the gun when it was smoking. What matters is who was holding it when it was fired. The police don't know because they didn't ask. Mr. Alexander doesn't know because the police didn't ask. And at the end of this trial, you won't know either because no one asked."

He took a breath, then brought it home. "And if you don't know, then you can't convict. At the end of this trial, the State will not have proved that Judge Hawkins pulled the trigger of that smoking gun, and it will then be your duty to return a verdict of not guilty. Thank you."

Raine returned to his seat, all eyes following him. Even Hawkins's. Especially Hawkins's.

"Nice job," he whispered to his attorney. "For a moment there, I thought you were going to include Trevor in your list of suspects."

"Nope. You said not to," Raine replied out of the corner of his mouth, "and you're the client."

Hawkins paused, then patted Raine on the shoulder. "Thanks."

"Mr. Alexander," Judge Wooten called down to the prosecutor. "You may call your first witness."

Alexander stood, but he seemed far less certain of himself than at the conclusion of his opening statement.

"The State calls," he announced, "Emil Szabo to the stand."

27

Raine knew a few things about trial practice. More than a few things, in fact. He knew the prosecution's first witness would be waiting in the hallway during opening statements. He knew Alexander had not prepared Emil Szabo for what Raine was going to ask him on cross-examination. And he knew Alexander didn't have time to do it before Szabo took the stand.

The prosecutor fetched Szabo from the hallway and pointed to the judge's bench to be sworn in. Szabo raised his right hand and swore to tell the truth, the whole truth, and nothing but the truth. Then he sat down on the witness stand, expecting to testify about nothing more than the memory of his dearly departed daughter.

"Could you please state your name for the record?" Alexander began the examination. He took up a neutral spot in the courtroom's 'well', standing in front of the prosecution table and slightly toward the jury box, to encourage his witness to deliver at least part of his answers to the jurors directly.

"Emil Szabo," he answered. He was dressed in a black suit with a silk tie of muted shades. He looked to be in mourning. An intentional choice, Raine was sure. Just like the decision that led to the need to mourn.

"Did you know a woman named Lydia Szabo?" Alexander asked next.

Szabo took a moment. He set his jaw, swallowed hard, and then answered, with the slightest hint of an accent, "Lydia was my daughter."

No tears, but an appropriate showing of emotion. What the jurors might expect from an older man.

Alexander then took him through the usual song and dance for the parent of a murder victim. Lydia's age, her hopes and dreams, a few of her more notable accomplishments, and finished with what was called the 'in-life photo': just a regular photo of Lydia while she was still alive, in contrast to the rest of the photographs of her lifeless body that would be shown to the jury. The in-life photo was always flattering, even when the victim was objectively a piece of crap. Lydia, on the other hand, had seemed like a genuinely nice person. Raine felt no heartburn when they showed the jury a picture of her on a sunny day in the park, her blonde hair blown back by the wind.

Alexander finished his examination with a sympathy-seeking, "Do you miss Lydia?"

"Every day," Szabo replied, his lips a hard line. "Every day."

"No further questions," Alexander announced.

It was Raine's turn.

"Any cross-examination, Mr. Raine?" Judge Wooten had to ask that, even though everyone in the courtroom knew the answer.

"Yes, Your Honor." Raine stood to reply to the judge, then stepped out from behind the defense table. He took up a position far closer to Szabo than Alexander had taken. Close enough to be obviously confrontational. Close enough for Szabo to see the still-healing cut on his eyebrow.

"You drive an Aston Martin, right?" Raine began. "A black Aston Martin sedan?"

"I own several cars," Szabo avoided answering directly. Raine didn't mind. A collection of luxury vehicles would trump a pool house.

"Including a black Aston Martin sedan?" Raine didn't let go.

Szabo sighed. "Yes," he admitted.

"You own several businesses, correct?" Raine jumped to the next topic.

"I own a company that owns several businesses," Szabo again avoided answering directly.

"Like a bunch of sketchy massage parlors, right?" Raine asserted.

"Objection!" Alexander rose to his feet. "That question violates at least three evidence rules. Rule 609, Rule 403, Rule 404(b). Probably more."

Judge Wooten frowned. "Mr. Raine?" he invited a response.

"I can rephrase the question," Raine offered.

"Please do so," Wooten replied.

Raine nodded, took a deep breath, then asked, "You traffic young girls from Asia as sex workers at those spas, don't you?"

The courtroom exploded again in gasps, not because of the topic—the spectators had already heard it—but because Raine actually went ahead and asked it like that.

Alexander stood again. "Objection, Your Honor. Same objection."

Raine looked to the judge. "It goes to motive, Your Honor."

Judge Wooten smiled at the development. He was clearly entertained.

"The only person's motive that's relevant, Your Honor," Alexander interjected, "is the defendant's."

"The motive that matters is the murderer's motive," Raine countered. "Just because Mr. Alexander wants the murderer to be Judge Hawkins doesn't mean that's true."

The judge chewed his cheek for a moment. Then he looked directly at Szabo. "Do you believe you can answer the question, Mr. Szabo?"

Szabo raised his thick, gray eyebrows. "Do I think I can answer whether I traffic young women for sex? Yes, I can answer that."

"Then answer it," Judge Wooten directed.

Alexander sat down, and Szabo locked eyes with Raine —which was good because it meant he wasn't looking at the jurors.

"No," Szabo declared. "I do not traffic anyone—girls, women, or men—from Asia or anywhere else to work as prostitutes in any of my businesses."

Szabo may have denied it, but everyone in the courtroom was thinking about it. And trying to decide whether to believe him. Raine would call that a win. Next topic.

"You were at the Hawkins residence at the time of your daughter's murder, correct?"

Szabo frowned. "Why would you say that?"

Raine actually appreciated Szabo's slipperiness. He hoped the jury was noticing it too.

"Because several of the people employed to work that night saw a man fitting your description arrive and depart in that black Aston Martin sedan you drove there. Oh, you also drove it to the Peony Spa in Georgetown a few weeks ago to rough up a young masseuse you definitely weren't trafficking for sex work."

"Objection again." Alexander was on his feet almost as much as Raine. "This is getting ridiculous."

Raine gestured at the witness. "He asked."

"It does seem like a compound question, Mr. Raine," Judge Wooten observed. "Or maybe a compound answer to the witness's question. In any event, please ask another question, rather than engaging in a freewheeling conversation with the witness."

Raine agreed and turned back to Szabo. "If I told you that the valet you tipped a hundred and fifty dollars remembers you and your Aston Martin, would you be willing to admit you were at the Hawkins residence the night Lydia was murdered?"

Szabo sighed through his nose. "I thought I was going to be testifying about Lydia, not about my whereabouts on the night of her murder."

"Your whereabouts on the night of her murder are about Lydia," Raine replied. "Now, I'll ask one more time, and if you avoid answering a third time, well, then, I think we all know the answer. You were at the Hawkins residence at the time of your daughter's death, weren't you?"

Szabo narrowed his eyes and gave Raine a look that made him think Szabo really wished Alexei had been able to finish the job at the spa.

"Yes," he finally admitted. "I went there to bring Lydia home. I knew she wasn't truly welcome in the Hawkins house. I was afraid Judge Hawkins would call his friends in the police department and have her arrested for trespassing."

That was a pretty good answer, Raine had to admit, although he didn't dare let the thought appear on his face. Still, it had taken Szabo three tries to think of it, so it lost some of its impact.

"I was told I wasn't on the guest list and asked to leave," Szabo continued. "I left before the gunshot."

"What gunshot?" Raine asked. "I didn't say anything about a gunshot."

"My daughter was shot to death, sir," Szabo growled back. "That means there was a gunshot."

"That's certainly part of what it means," Raine agreed.

He took a moment then to return to the defense table and extract something from his briefcase. The button he found in the ivy, sealed inside a small Ziploc baggie. "I have one more line of inquiry, Mr. Szabo."

Raine handed the baggie to the bailiff and had him mark it as an exhibit. He then showed the new exhibit to his opponent, as required by the court rules. Alexander frowned at it, but didn't say anything. There wasn't anything for him to object to. Not yet anyway.

"I like your suit," Raine said to Szabo, turning back to approach the witness stand. "I'm guessing that's not off the rack, is it?"

"It is not," Szabo confirmed.

"Do you have a particular tailor who makes your suits?" Raine asked.

"I have one who makes most of them, yes," Szabo answered.

Raine stepped forward and handed Szabo the baggie

with the button in it. "You should tell him to do a better job sewing the buttons on. Do you recognize that?"

Szabo held the baggie up by its top edge and peered at the object within. "It appears to be a plastic button."

"A plastic button from one of your suits, perhaps?" Raine suggested. "What would you say if I told you this button was recovered from the ivy on a lattice immediately outside the window of the study where Lydia was murdered?"

"I would say," Szabo extended the bag back to Raine, "that it's someone else's button. My tailor doesn't use cheap plastic buttons for my suits. My suits have buttons of shell, horn, or even metal. Never plastic."

Raine was reminded of the old advice to never ask a question you don't already know the answer to. The problem wasn't so much Szabo's answer as how believable it was.

He raised his arm and pointed to the buttons affixed to the end of his sleeve. "See? These are genuine mother-of-pearl."

Raine didn't need to look to know he was telling the truth. But the jurors all looked. It was time to sit down. "No further questions, Your Honor."

Raine walked back to take his seat behind the defense table.

Hawkins slid over his notepad on which he'd written, 'Nice Job.' He'd obviously written it before the button gambit.

Alexander stood even as the judge asked him, "Any redirect-examination, counsel?"

"Yes, Your Honor," Alexander confirmed. He stepped forward into the well again. "I hate to ask this, Mr. Szabo, but defense counsel has forced my hand. Did you murder your own daughter, sir?"

STEPHEN PENNER

"I absolutely did not," Szabo boomed. "And it is beyond offensive to suggest I could ever do that."

"No further questions," Alexander declared and returned to his seat.

"Any recross-examination, Mr. Raine?" Judge Wooten invited.

Raine took a moment. Recross was limited to whatever the prosecutor had asked on redirect, and that had been only one question. Szabo was hardly going to suddenly crack on the stand and confess to the murder. So, Raine decided to ask him that.

"And if you did murder your daughter because she threatened to expose your sex-trafficking operation, you certainly wouldn't admit to that right here and now in open court, would you?"

Alexander objected again.

Raine withdrew the question before Wooten had a chance to rule on the objection. It wasn't the answer that mattered. It was the question. The jury had heard that, and that was enough. "No further questions."

"May this witness be excused?" Judge Wooten seemed pleased to get to ask.

If both lawyers said yes, then Szabo would not testify again and could sit in on the remainder of the proceedings. If either lawyer said no, then Szabo would be subject to being recalled to the stand without the necessity of a new subpoena. That would mean he was still a witness and couldn't watch the trial.

"The State would excuse the witness," Alexander answered.

But Raine wasn't about to let the old man sit through the trial, intimidating or otherwise impacting the jurors.

Besides, Raine wasn't done with him. When it came time for Raine to put on the defense case, Emil Szabo would again be one of the first witnesses. "No, Your Honor. The defense asks that the witness remain subject to recall."

"Very well," Wooten replied. "You are free to leave now, Mr. Szabo, but you may be recalled to testify at a later time."

Szabo forced a pained smile. "Wonderful." Then he stood up and exited the courtroom.

Judge Wooten waited for the door to close behind Szabo, then looked down at the prosecutor. "Please call your next witness, Mr. Alexander."

It was going to be a long trial.

28

The next set of witnesses were a parade of the fundraiser attendees who had rushed in to find Hawkins standing over Lydia's body, with four notable exceptions: Raine and his investigator, whom the prosecution were not allowed to call as witnesses, and Cindy and Trevor, whom Alexander was saving for last.

That left nine witnesses to work through. Alexander called them in alphabetical order. Janine Allred, Timothy Davis, etc. Each had a different, although similar, reason for being invited to Hawkins's fundraiser. Two things they all had in common were that Hawkins had asked them for money, and none of them gave him any after they saw what they thought he had done.

Raine's cross-examination of each witness consisted of the same three questions:

"When you heard the gunshot, you were outside the study, correct?"

"You did not see who actually fired the gunshot that killed Lydia Szabo, correct?"

"You can't say that Judge Hawkins didn't pick the gun up off the floor after the real killer dropped it and fled, can you?"

It wasn't as dramatic as the cross-examination of Emil Szabo, but it was important. Alexander had nine witnesses tell the jury that Hawkins was holding the smoking gun. Raine walked up to all nine of them and asked, 'So what?'

The guests were followed by a smaller group of the contractors hired to work at the Hawkins residence the night of the murder. Most of them had little of value to offer the jury. But Alexander knew if he failed to call even one of the witnesses identified by police, Raine would stand up in closing argument and accuse him of intentionally not calling Champagne Tray Carrier #3 or Rich Potential Donor #7 because they would have said something that would have helped the defense. And Alexander was right. Raine absolutely would have done that. It was his job.

Szabo's admission that he was at the Hawkinses' the night of the murder impacted the number and focus of Raine's questions. He no longer needed to convince the jurors that the rich older man the valets and caterers saw was Emil Szabo. Szabo had admitted as much. Instead, Raine trained his questioning on the details Szabo had offered to explain away his presence there, and any involvement in the gunshot that took his daughter's life.

When Marcus the valet testified that he remembered seeing a man matching Szabo's description, Raine had him describe the man's demeanor rather than his appearance.

"You were surprised by how calm the man was, weren't you?"

"Well, yeah, a little," Marcus answered. "Everybody else

was freaking out. It was a gunshot, you know? But he didn't react at all."

"Like he was used to gunshots, maybe?" Raine suggested.

"Sure, I guess," Marcus nominally agreed.

"Or he expected it," Raine posited.

Marcus's eyes widened a bit at that. "Oh. Yeah. Maybe."

"Or maybe both," Raine said.

Marcus nodded. "Yeah, both."

Then, when Simone, the other valet, testified seeing the same man and receiving $150 in tips from him, Raine leaned into the timing of it all.

"He wanted his car to be on site, not up the street, isn't that right?"

"Yes," Simone answered. "That's exactly what he wanted."

"Like a robber making sure he has a getaway car right outside the bank?" Raine offered the analogy.

Simone nodded. "Yeah, I guess so."

"And when he came to get into the getaway car," Raine continued, "he was calm and focused, even though everyone else was panicked by the gunshot. Correct?"

Simone thought for a moment. "You know, I think he might have walked up right as the gunshot happened. But you're right. He wasn't bothered by it at all."

Raine fought off a frown. "You think he was already outside when the gunshot went off?"

Simone took a few moments to consider. "I don't remember for sure, but yeah. I think he was walking up to the valet stand when the shot went off. Everyone started screaming, but he just handed me a hundred and asked me to get his car first."

That frown was pushing itself onto Raine's face despite what it would communicate to the jurors. "Do you recall telling me and my investigator earlier that the gunshot happened first and then the man appeared?"

Simone shook her head. "I don't think I would have said that. I probably said something like he was calm when everyone else was panicking after the gunshot. But I'm pretty sure he was already outside when we heard the shot."

Raine suppressed a wince. "But you could be wrong about that," he tried. "Right?"

Simone shrugged. "Maybe. But probably not."

When Linda, the head caterer, testified that she was in charge of the guest list, Raine used it to cast doubt on one of Szabo's key assertions as to his movements that evening.

"Emil Szabo was not on the guest list," Linda confirmed Raine's inquiry.

"Do you ever recall a man matching Mr. Szabo's description trying to enter the front of the home by way of the guest list?" Raine asked.

"I do not," Linda answered.

"Do you think you would remember that?"

"I would."

"And did you see a man like that leave the house through the front door," Raine asked, "perhaps immediately after the gunshot?"

"It got crazy pretty quick when that gunshot went off," Linda explained, "but I saw everyone who rushed out that front door and I didn't see anyone like that."

And when Linda's son, Jimmy, all sixteen years of him, testified, Raine had him provide the jury with Szabo's entrance.

"Did you see an older man with gray hair and a nice suit enter the home through the back door?" Raine asked him.

"Um, yes," Jimmy answered quietly.

"Did you see him leave the same way?"

"Um, no."

"Did you ever see him again after he snuck into the home?"

"Um, no."

That left the off-duty cops. Raine had no illusions that either of them would willfully help Hawkins. But he could have fun with them anyway. Especially Sokolowski.

Alexander called Corporal Turner first. Turner insisted he didn't see anything or anyone suspicious the entire night until suddenly there was a gunshot, and he ran inside to find Hawkins standing over the body. All of the witnesses said Hawkins was holding the gun when they rushed in. They arrested Hawkins, and that was it.

Raine didn't spend much time with Turner. There was really only one question he wanted the jury to hear.

"You just testified that you didn't see anything suspicious the entire night leading up to a murder," Raine pointed out. "Now, is that because you're incompetent, or because you're scared to death of Emil Szabo?"

Turner's answer didn't matter. He stumbled and sputtered through a denial of either of the options Raine had presented. But again, it was the question that mattered.

And then, finally, Alexander called Officer Jim Sokolowski to the stand.

Sokolowski marched into the courtroom with his chin up and his expression dutifully serious. He was in his light blue dress uniform, just like Turner's but without the stripes. He raised his right hand and swore to tell the truth, the whole truth, and nothing but the truth. Everyone but Raine believed him.

"Please state your name for the record," Alexander began his examination.

"James Andrew Sokolowski." He turned to deliver his answer to the jury, just like he'd been trained to do at the academy.

"How are you employed, sir?" Alexander continued the standard name-rank-and-serial-number introduction of the examination.

"I'm a police officer with the Seattle Police Department." Again, directly to the jurors, with a flash of a smile.

"How long have you been a police officer with the Seattle Police Department?"

"Twelve years next May," he answered. "A long time."

Raine could agree that was a long time to be a cop. No wonder he'd gone bad.

"What are your current duties and assignment?" Alexander seemed like he was trying to force some life into the early part of his examination, but some questions are just too basic to be anything but boring.

"I am a patrol officer," Sokolowski explained to the jurors. "I respond to calls and actively patrol looking for illegal activity. My current assignment is day shift, Queen Sector Two, West Precinct."

"Is that the Magnolia neighborhood?" Alexander translated.

"Yes," Sokolowski confirmed.

"Okay, let's talk about the incident in this case," Alexander moved to his next area of inquiry. "Were you one of the officers who eventually effectuated an arrest of the defendant on suspicion of murder?"

"I was," Sokolowski confirmed.

"And that occurred at the defendant's home; is that correct?"

"Yes, that is correct," Sokolowski answered.

"Is the defendant's home in your sector?" Alexander asked. "That is, is it in the Magnolia neighborhood?"

Again, a nod to the jurors. "It is."

"Is that why you were there to make the arrest?" Alexander asked. "Were you on duty that night?"

"I was working," Sokolowski explained, "but I wasn't on duty. I was working an off-duty security detail at the defendant's home."

"The defendant hired you as security for an event at his home?" Alexander asked.

"Yes, exactly," Sokolowski confirmed.

"What was the event?"

"I believe it was a political fundraiser of some sort," Sokolowski answered. "Judge Hawkins is, well, a judge. He has to run for reelection every four years. I guess the event was related to that."

"Were you the only off-duty police officer working security at the fundraiser?" Alexander continued.

"No. Corporal Turner was also working the fundraiser," Sokolowski answered. "It was the two of us."

"And how did you divide up the duties?" Alexander asked. "Was one of you securing the front door while the other searched everyone for weapons?"

"Oh no, no. Nothing like that," Sokolowski waved the ideas away. "No, we were supposed to be very low-key. Almost invisible. Mostly we walked the perimeter of the property and made sure people checked in with the person at the front door who had the guest list."

"Do you know why the defendant felt the need to hire two off-duty police officers to protect his event?" Alexander asked.

"I do now," Sokolowski replied. "I didn't then, though."

"Why?" Alexander prompted. "If you know."

"Apparently, Judge Hawkins's son got into some trouble with a local family with a lot of business interests here in town," Sokolowski answered. "I don't know all the details. I think the son was dating the daughter of the other family. Anyway, I guess Judge Hawkins was afraid the other family might come over and commit some sort of violence or something."

"And did they?" Alexander asked.

Sokolowski thought for a moment. "There was violence that night, but it didn't come from that other family. In fact, their daughter was the victim. The violence came from Judge Hawkins."

"What was the nature of that violence?" Alexander invited.

Sokolowski turned again to the jurors, but there was no charming smile that time. Just a grim expression, and the declaration, "He murdered her."

Alexander took Sokolowski through the rest of the evening. Perimeter patrols and half-hourly check-ins with Turner. It was an easy gig until it wasn't. There was a gunshot. He ran inside, found Hawkins standing over Lydia, just like Turner had described. They tackled him, hand-cuffed him, secured the immediate scene, and called for the homicide team to come out.

"At any point, did you see the victim's father, Emil Szabo, anywhere on the property that night?" Alexander brought his questioning to a close.

"I did not," Sokolowski told the jurors. "That doesn't mean he wasn't there. I just never saw him."

"Thank you, Officer Sokolowski." Alexander nodded to his witness. "I have no further questions for you."

Judge Wooten leaned forward and peered down at Raine. "Cross-examination?" he invited.

Oh, yeah, Raine thought. "Yes, Your Honor," he said.

He stepped out from behind his table and strode right up to Sokolowski. He was definitely too close. Sokolowski pushed back in his seat slightly. He was obviously uncomfortable. So was everyone watching.

"You're on Emil Szabo's payroll, aren't you?" Raine saw no reason to dance around the subject.

"What?" Sokolowski gasped. "No. No, of course not."

"But you know him?" Raine continued. "So, personally? Are you friends with the man?"

Sokolowski shook his head and looked around the courtroom, a bit nervously, Raine thought. "I am not friends with Emil Szabo."

Raine stepped away from the front of the witness stand. He raised a thoughtful hand to his lips and nodded a few times as he paced several steps away, then turned back to confront the witness again. "Then why were you seen at one of his spas, the Peony Spa in Georgetown, far outside of your sector, shaking hands with him?"

"What?" Sokolowski forced a laugh. "When? I don't remember anything like that ever happening."

"It was the same day Mr. Szabo assaulted one of the young women he had forced into prostitution at that spa," Raine prompted. "Although I doubt that was ever reported to the police."

"Your Honor," Alexander stood up to interrupt, "I am

going to object to this line of questioning. The witness has answered that he did not have any such interaction with Mr. Szabo. At this point, Mr. Raine is merely badgering the witness and trying to make speeches with his questions."

"Your Honor," Raine responded, "I am not merely doing those things. I am also pursuing a relevant line of inquiry regarding the potential bias of this witness, as well as laying the foundation to call my investigator to the stand to show that he is lying about his rendezvous with Emil Szabo."

"Oh, uh, actually," Sokolowski spoke up before Judge Wooten could rule. "I do remember meeting Mr. Szabo that time."

Raine sighed. Alexander's objection had given Sokolowski time to think of a way to explain it away. Especially after he realized he would be caught in a lie if he didn't come up with something.

"I will withdraw my objection," Alexander offered, and he sat down again.

"You may continue, Mr. Raine," Judge Wooten invited.

Raine sighed again, but he had to ask. "You remember meeting with Emil Szabo now? Now that you realize I have a witness who saw you?"

"It took me a moment to remember because you made it sound like we were friends or something," Sokolowski attempted to explain, "and that meeting wasn't like a friend thing."

"It was like a getting paid off thing?" Raine suggested.

"No," Sokolowski protested. But then, "Well, yes. I mean, I got paid. But it was just another off-duty gig. He hired me to do a quick off-duty security job. Just like Judge Hawkins did."

Raine had to hand it to Sokolowski. That was about as

good an explanation as he could create. "And I'm sure you don't remember the details of that job now, do you?" he ventured.

Sokolowski shook his head and shrugged. "No, I'm afraid not. It was something really small. I don't even remember where it was."

"Of course you don't," Raine sneered. He considered whether it was worth questioning Sokolowski any further. It was obvious to him that Sokolowski had just lied under oath. He would just have to hope it was obvious to at least some of the jurors as well. Giving him more airtime to flash charming smiles at them wasn't going to help Raine any. "No further questions."

Alexander had no redirect-examination. He obviously knew he needed to get Sokolowski off the stand as soon as possible. Sokolowski was excused.

Judge Wooten looked at the clock on the courtroom wall. "It's getting late in the day," he observed. "Is your next witness brief, Mr. Alexander?"

"My next witness is not brief, Your Honor," Alexander answered. "It will be the lead detective on the case. I do not believe we could finish his testimony before the end of the day today."

Judge Wooten looked to Raine.

"I would agree with that, Your Honor," Raine offered. "The defense would not object to adjourning for the day and starting with the detective fresh in the morning."

That would also give Raine extra time to prepare for one of the most important witnesses in the trial.

"Very well. We will reconvene at nine o'clock tomorrow morning," the judge agreed. He banged his gavel on the bench. "Court is adjourned."

As the courtroom began to empty, Hawkins leaned over to Raine. "Nice job with the cop today. Any chance you can do that again to the detective?"

Raine frowned. "I hope not. That would mean he's on Szabo's payroll too."

29

The next morning, Alexander stood to announce, "The State calls Detective Kevin Ewing to the stand."

Raine had no reason to believe Ewing was also working for Szabo, although he hadn't had a reason to think that about Sokolowski until he saw them together. Raine was unlikely to convince the jurors that Ewing was dirty. But that was okay. He only needed to convince them he might have made a mistake. Even lead detectives were only human.

"Please state your name for the record," Alexander began again with the same directive he gave every witness.

"Kevin Ewing." He was wearing a dark green blazer that didn't go well with his navy blue pants. A wrinkled white dress shirt tried in vain to pull the outfit together.

"How are you employed, sir?"

"I'm a detective with the Seattle Police Department."

"How long have you been a detective with the Seattle Police Department?" Alexander moved along.

"I've been with the department for fifteen years," Ewing answered. "I've been a detective for almost three years now."

"What kind of crimes do you investigate?" Alexander asked next.

"I recently moved from property crimes to major crimes," Ewing answered.

"Does major crimes include murder?" Alexander asked, if a bit unnecessarily.

Ewing nodded. "Yes, sir, it does."

"Were you involved in the investigation of the murder of Lydia Szabo at the residence of the defendant?"

"I was," Ewing confirmed. "I was the lead detective."

"And what does a lead detective do in a murder investigation?" Alexander prompted.

"Well, the first thing is, I responded to the scene." Ewing turned to deliver his answer to the jury.

"What did you do when you arrived at the scene?" Alexander continued his examination.

"Well, when I first arrived, I was briefed by the off-duty officers who had been working security at the event," Ewing answered. "They explained they heard a single gunshot, and when they entered the room where the victim was, they observed the victim on the floor, lying in a large pool of blood from a single gunshot wound to the head."

"Did they tell you whether there was anyone else in the room when they arrived?" Alexander asked.

"They reported that there were several witnesses who all saw the defendant," Ewing pointed at Hawkins, "standing over the victim with a pistol in his hand."

Raine could have objected. What the witnesses told the officers was hearsay. What the officers told the detective the witnesses told them was double hearsay. But all of those witnesses had already testified. Raine wouldn't be preventing the information from getting to the jury. And he had already told the jurors that it didn't matter what they saw after the gunshot because none of them saw the gunshot itself. At best, objecting would have made him look pedantic. At worst, it would have made him seem worried about what those witnesses saw after all.

"Was the pistol still smoking?" Alexander harkened back to his opening statement.

"Uh, I'm not sure about that," Ewing admitted. "Modern firearms don't produce as much smoke as the old-fashioned revolvers you see in movies, but they do produce some. Still, actual smoke wasn't really necessary. A dozen people ran into the room within seconds of hearing a gunshot and saw the defendant standing over the victim with the murder weapon in his hand. I didn't need to know there was smoke coming out of the barrel to know he had fired the fatal shot."

That was exactly the kind of jumping to conclusions Raine told the jurors they could expect from the cops. It was nice of Ewing to confirm it at the beginning of his testimony.

Alexander took Ewing through the rest of his investigation, such as it was. He interviewed everyone there that night, attended the autopsy, and sent the gun and bullet to the lab for processing. Everything pointed to Hawkins as the murderer. Case closed.

"No further questions, Your Honor," Alexander announced upon completion of his examination.

Judge Wooten then invited Raine to cross-examine. He accepted.

"I have two main areas of inquiry, Detective Ewing," Raine said to orient his witness and the jury.

"Okay," Ewing replied with narrowed eyes and a hint of suspicion in his voice.

"First, the night of the murder," Raine began. "You interviewed everyone who was there at the time of the gunshot. Is that right?"

Ewing frowned slightly. "Theoretically, some people may have left before officers arrived to lock down the scene, so I can't say I spoke to everyone who was there when the gunshot occurred. I can say I spoke to everyone who was there and also remained on scene until police arrived. That seemed to be almost everyone. There were a lot of people."

"And you spoke with all of them?" Raine asked.

"I did," Ewing confirmed.

"You asked them what they observed that might be helpful to your investigation, right?"

"Yes," Ewing answered.

"But by the time you did that," Raine pointed out, "you had already arrested Judge Hawkins for the murder, isn't that true?"

Ewing hesitated before answering. "Sometimes you need to move quickly to arrest a suspect before he flees or hurts someone else. You can't wait hours while you interview dozens of people, most of whom didn't see anything of value anyway."

"Ah." Raine raised a finger into the air. "And you know they didn't see anything of value because most of them didn't run upstairs and see your suspect holding the murder weapon. Is that what you're saying?"

Ewing shifted in his chair. "Not exactly. Obviously, if they had additional information—"

"Or differing information," Raine interjected.

"Or differing information, sure," Ewing accepted, "then we would want to know that."

"But how would they know to tell you that additional, perhaps differing information," Raine put to him, "if you didn't ask for it, because you had already made up your mind that Judge Hawkins was guilty?"

"Now, see, that's not accurate," Ewing protested.

"Where was Judge Hawkins while you conducted these other interviews?" Raine demanded. "Where was he for the hours and hours it took you to talk to everyone? He was handcuffed and in the back of a patrol car, wasn't he? He was taken downtown and booked into the jail before you finished even half of those interviews, isn't that right?"

"Objection," Alexander called out. "Compound question."

"There do seem to be a lot of questions in there, counsel," Judge Wooten agreed. "I have to sustain that objection."

"Understood, Your Honor," Raine replied. "I'll break it down so even a new major crimes detective can understand. When you interviewed these witnesses as part of your investigation, you had already arrested and booked your suspect, isn't that right?"

Ewing's mouth was a tight line. "Investigations can take longer than the amount of time we have to effectuate an arrest. We have to address flight risk and danger to others."

"So, that's a yes," Raine translated. "When you were deciding what questions to ask these witnesses, you had already arrested a sitting judge for murder. How much trouble would you have been in if you'd arrested a judge only to have witnesses tell you someone else might have committed the murder?"

Ewing grinned slightly and shook his head at Raine. "None of the witnesses said that."

"Because you were afraid to ask," Raine accused. "For example, did you ask any of them if they saw Emil Szabo come to the event at approximately the same time as the murder?"

"Emil Szabo?" Ewing repeated the name. "The victim's father?"

"Oh good, you do know him," Raine said. "Well, then let's go ahead and move on to my second area of inquiry. As a major crimes detective, are you aware that Emil Szabo is running a human trafficking ring out of his spas?"

"Objection!" Alexander sprang again to his feet. "This is really going too far, Your Honor."

"I would think it's relevant," Raine argued to Wooten, "if this detective is aware that a possible suspect not only is engaged in criminal activity of the vilest kind, but also lied about it when he testified in this very trial."

Judge Wooten seemed less entertained than he had been when Raine had confronted Szabo directly. "I think you've made your point, Mr. Raine. Do you have any other questions, or may this witness be excused?"

"Just one more area of inquiry, Your Honor," Raine answered. He hadn't made every point he wanted to make.

Raine turned back to Ewing. "You don't know whether any of the windows in the study were open, isn't that right?"

"The windows?" Ewing questioned. "Um, no, not off the top of my head."

"Yeah, not in your crime scene photos either," Raine pointed out. "But why check the windows when the killer was caught inside the room, right?"

Ewing took a moment, then nodded. "Right."

"Unless," Raine raised a finger, "oops, someone else committed the murder and maybe jumped out the window? Maybe left some small article of clothing behind in the ivy on the trellis?"

Ewing didn't have a reply for Raine's suggestions.

"Do you see," Raine asked him, "how jumping to the conclusion that Judge Hawkins was guilty might have impacted your investigation?"

"I do not believe my investigation was compromised," Ewing insisted.

"I'm sure you don't," Raine replied. "That's part of the problem, too. No further questions."

Alexander had no redirect-examination, and Detective Ewing was excused. His testimony had taken long enough that Wooten took the morning recess for the court reporter's hands to rest. Raine decided to take the opportunity to visit the restroom. He'd had two cups of coffee before court began.

But almost as soon as he stepped into the hallway, he was accosted by Detective Ewing.

"Come with me." He grabbed Raine by the elbow and steered him around the corner where no one else was. Raine wondered if Ewing was going to try to rough him up. He felt comfortable he could take the detective, as long as no guns or tasers were pulled.

"What's wrong, Detective?" Raine asked, extracting his arm from Ewing's grip. "Did I hit a little too close to home about your inadequate investigation?"

"No," Ewing barked. Then he glanced all around and lowered his voice. "You need to back off Emil Szabo."

Raine couldn't believe what he was hearing. "Are you on his payroll too?"

"What? No! I'm not on his payroll," Ewing rebuked. "That's not what I mean. What I mean is, if you keep pushing on this, you could ruin six months of undercover work. Stay out of it."

30

After calling the ballistics expert to confirm the murder weapon belonged to Hawkins and the medical examiner to confirm Lydia died from a single gunshot wound to the head—facts which were not in doubt—Alexander had two witnesses left before he rested his case: Trevor Hawkins and Cindy Hawkins.

Professionally, Raine agreed with the decision to call them last. Alexander could hardly not call them at all; that would make the jury think he was scared of what they had to say. More importantly, to the extent that they also witnessed Hawkins standing over Lydia's body, there was no more dramatic way to finish the prosecution's case than to have the defendant's own wife and child reaffirm that Hawkins was holding the smoking gun.

Personally, Raine disliked it. But not as much as Hawkins did.

"I hate that they have to testify," Hawkins moaned as they sat at the defense counsel just before court reconvened. "This is already too much for them. Especially Cindy."

"I know." Raine placed a hand on his friend's back. "It'll be fine, and then it'll be over. Maybe Alexander will make Cindy cry and the jury will hate him. Think positive."

Hawkins frowned at his lawyer. "My wife crying in open court is not a positive thought."

Raine was about to defend his remark when the bailiff stood and announced the recommencement of the proceedings, "All rise! The King County Superior Court is now in session, The Honorable Frank Wooten, visiting judge, presiding."

Wooten took his seat on the bench and gazed down at the lawyers. "Are the parties ready to proceed?"

"The State is ready, Your Honor," Alexander answered. "We have two final witnesses, and then we will rest our case."

Wooten nodded. "Very good." A glance at the defense table.

"The defense is ready as well, Your Honor," Raine confirmed.

Wooten nodded, then instructed the bailiff, "Bring in the jurors."

A few short minutes later, the jury was in the jury box, and the trial was ready to proceed.

"You may call your next witness, Mr. Alexander," Judge Wooten invited.

Alexander stood to declare, with all the drama the announcement very much warranted, "The State calls Trevor Hawkins to the stand."

Alexander personally walked to the courtroom doors and brought Trevor inside. Cindy would wait out in the hallway. Witnesses couldn't listen to each other testify, even if they were mother and son. Judge Wooten stood

and bade Trevor to approach the bench and be
sworn in.

"Raise your right hand," the judge instructed as he did
the same. "Do you solemnly swear to tell the truth, the
whole truth, and nothing but the truth?"

Trevor nodded, swallowed, and croaked, "I do."

"Please take the witness stand," Judge Wooten directed.

Trevor walked slowly to the stand and sat down. He was
wearing a blue button-up dress shirt with no jacket, black
pants that looked too small for him, and a pair of black
shoes that looked too big for him. His eyes were set into dark
circles, and they darted around the courtroom.

Alexander slowly approached the witness stand. "Please
state your name for the record."

"Uh, Trevor. Trevor Hawkins," he stammered.

"How old are you, Mr. Hawkins?"

"I'm, um, I'm twenty-two years old," Trevor answered.

Trevor's voice faltered. His shirt already had sweat stains
at the armpits.

"Do you know the defendant, Michael Hawkins?"
Alexander asked, with a gesture toward the defense table.

Hawkins smiled awkwardly at his son.

Trevor nodded. "He's my dad."

Alexander took a moment, not to emphasize his last
question, but to make sure he had everyone's attention for
the next one. "And did you know Lydia Szabo?"

Trevor hesitated. He looked down, then up, then at the
jury, then at his father. When he looked back at Alexander,
his eyes were glistening. "Yes."

Raine was glad for the show of emotion. He needed
Trevor to be upset that his girlfriend was murdered, but not
angry at his father—because he didn't do it. Raine doubted

Alexander would construct his questioning to elicit those particular sentiments, but he certainly would on cross. Alexander didn't seem to mind the emotion either. After all, Trevor's girlfriend had been murdered. He was a victim too, after a fashion. "How did you know Lydia?"

Trevor sighed and dropped his gaze again. "She was my girlfriend."

"How long was she your girlfriend?"

"About six months," Trevor answered.

"So, it was starting to get serious?" Alexander suggested.

Trevor shrugged. "I guess. Maybe. I'm not sure."

Alexander nodded a few times and raised a hand to his chin, ostensibly thinking of his next question. Raine knew he had every last one of his questions memorized. "There's been some talk about you owing some money to someone in Lydia's family. Is that accurate?"

Trevor's moist eyes widened and his cheeks flared pink. "Um..."

"I'll remind you that you're under oath, Mr. Hawkins," Alexander said.

"Yes," Trevor admitted. "I, uh, I borrowed some money from her brother. See, I couldn't find a job when I graduated from college. I was living with my parents. I still am. And anyway, you know, there were just things I needed to spend money on, and I thought... well, I don't know what I was thinking. But yes. I owe her brother some money."

"A lot of money?" Alexander asked.

Trevor hesitated again, then admitted. "Yeah. A lot."

"How much?"

"Too much," Trevor answered. "I couldn't pay it back. It kind of became a problem."

"Between you and Lydia?" Alexander suggested.

"Yeah," Trevor confirmed. "And other ways too."

"Okay." Another series of nods from Alexander. He took a few steps to the side, ready to launch into his next area of inquiry. "Let's talk about the night she was murdered. Were you there?"

"Was I there when she was shot?" Trevor asked, eyes widening again. They had dried out. "No. No, definitely not."

Alexander shook his head. "No, I mean, were you at your parents' house that night in general? Were you at the fundraiser?"

"Oh." Trevor let out an audible exhale. "I was at the house, but I wasn't really at the fundraiser. I was living there, but we converted the pool house into, like, an apartment. I hung out there most of the night. I didn't really want to hang out with a bunch of lawyers and judges." He jerked his head up at Wooten. "No offense."

"None taken." Alexander smiled politely. "Did you spend the entire night in the pool house then? Did you ever come inside?"

"I mean, I came inside to get some food," Trevor admitted, "and use the bathroom. There's no bathroom in the pool house. That's kind of annoying, actually. But yeah, other than that, I stayed out back."

"What about Lydia?" Alexander asked. "Was she there that night?"

Trevor frowned and nodded. "Yeah."

"And did she hang out with you in the pool house, or was she inside with all of those lawyers and judges?"

"A little bit of both," Trevor answered. "We were hanging out at my place for a while, but..." he trailed off.

"But what?" Alexander prompted.

"We had a little argument," Trevor admitted. "Nothing

too serious. Just the same old thing we usually argued about."

"And what was that?" Alexander inquired.

"Money," Trevor answered. "Me getting a job. Paying back her brother. Her dad and my dad and everything that was happening."

Raine leaned forward. He wondered whether Alexander would go down that road and get into how Szabo was trying to blackmail Hawkins. It was a rabbit hole, but it was also motive.

He went there. "What was your understanding of the issue between Lydia's father and your father?"

"Um, well." Trevor shifted in his seat. "I guess there was some case where, like, Lydia's dad's company broke some laws or something. He wanted my dad to be the judge and dismiss it. If my dad agreed, then he'd forget about what I owed Lydia's brother. But if he didn't..."

"If he didn't, then what would happen?" Alexander prodded him.

"I mean, I'm not totally sure," Trevor qualified, "but I guess maybe they would, like, break my knees or something. Like loan-shark stuff, I guess."

"Did you think that would really happen?" Alexander asked.

Trevor shrugged. "I don't know."

"Did your father think it would happen?" Alexander followed up.

Raine could have objected as speculation, but he decided to let Trevor answer the question. If he could.

"I think so," Trevor answered. "He and my mom seemed pretty nervous about it. They were trying to figure out what to do, I think. But they didn't really involve me. That's just kind of how they've always been with me."

Probably why Trevor ended up moving back home, Raine thought, but he didn't say it aloud.

"Did your father seem angry about it?" Alexander suggested.

"Angry?" Trevor considered. "I wouldn't say 'angry'. More like stressed."

"Stressed?"

"Yeah."

"Okay," Alexander accepted the characterization. "Did he ever say anything about talking to Lydia about it?"

"Lydia? No," Trevor answered. "I don't think he would have talked to her directly about it."

"Why do you say that?"

"Because when I suggested that, he shot it down," Trevor answered. "I said she could help us out. Talk to her brother and her dad. But my parents didn't want to do that."

"Why not?" Alexander questioned.

"I don't think they trusted her."

"But you did?" Alexander asked.

Trevor took a little too long to answer, but asserted, "Yes. I trusted her."

Alexander took a few steps back toward his original position, then pressed ahead with his examination. "Let's talk about the timeline when Lydia was shot and killed. Do you recall hearing a gunshot inside the home?"

Trevor's expression faltered again. His lower lip shook slightly. He nodded. "Yes."

"Were you inside the house or out in the pool house?"

"I was inside the house," Trevor answered. "I came back in for more food. That was basically my dinner that night."

"So, you were in the kitchen?"

"I think I had left the kitchen and was just kind of walking around," Trevor explained. "I was looking for Lydia. I wanted to make up after our argument."

"Was she anywhere to be seen?" Alexander asked.

"Well, no," Trevor answered.

"Because she was upstairs," Alexander said.

"Yeah."

"And then you heard the gunshot?"

"Yes."

"What did you do?" Alexander asked.

"I dropped my plate and ran upstairs," Trevor answered.

"Now why would you do that?" Alexander questioned. "Why wouldn't you run the other way, away from the gunshot?"

Trevor thought for a moment. "I guess because I knew my dad kept a gun in his desk and I was afraid something bad had happened to him."

That was a nice answer, Raine supposed.

"So, you ran directly to your father's study?" Alexander asked.

"Yes," Trevor confirmed.

"And what did you see?" Alexander demanded. "Tell the jury exactly what you saw."

Trevor hesitated. He looked at his father again.

Hawkins nodded to him. "Go ahead, son," he whispered.

"I saw Lydia on the floor," Trevor answered. "She was bleeding from her head. And my dad was standing over her, holding his gun."

Alexander nodded. He took a moment, then clasped his hands together. "Thank you, Mr. Hawkins. I have no further questions for you."

It was Raine's turn.

"Any cross-examination, Mr. Raine?" Judge Wooten asked.

"Yes, Your Honor." Raine stood up and stepped out from behind the defense table. "Hello, Trevor."

Trevor nodded back to him. "Hello, Mr. Raine."

"I'm not going to ask you a lot of questions," Raine assured him. "But I do have a few things I want to talk with you about."

"Okay." Trevor didn't seem to relax any from the change in questioners. He was still sweating noticeably, his brown curls sticking to his neck.

"You said your dad didn't really talk to you about what his plan was to deal with the money you owed the Szabos," Raine recalled. "But he did seem to have a plan, right? Even if he didn't tell you what it was."

"It seemed like they were still trying to work it out," Trevor answered.

"Okay," Raine allowed, "but no one was talking about killing anyone, right?"

"What?" Trevor gasped. "Oh, no. No, of course not."

"And certainly not Lydia, right?" Raine followed up. "I mean, you thought she could even help you, right?"

"Right," Trevor agreed immediately.

"Okay, let's talk about what you did and where you were the night of the murder," Raine said. "You mentioned earlier that you and Lydia had an argument; is that right?"

Trevor sighed. He raised his arm and ran a hand through his hair. "Yeah," he answered and started to explain, but Raine didn't hear the answer. He was staring at Trevor's arm.

After a few moments, Judge Wooten had to prompt him. "Mr. Raine? Do you have another question?"

Raine jerked his head up at the judge. "Um. Yes. I mean, no. I mean... Can I have a moment, Your Honor?"

Wooten's eyebrows knitted together, but he nodded. "A moment," he allowed.

Raine hurried back to the defense table and leaned across it to whisper in Hawkins's ear. "His shirt. The cuff."

"What about it?" Hawkins whispered back.

Raine took a moment to be certain he saw what he'd seen. "The button is missing."

Hawkins leaned back and looked at Raine, his expression horrified. He looked past Raine at his son, and back to Raine. Then he sprang to his feet.

"I plead guilty, Your Honor!" Hawkins shouted up at Judge Wooten. "I want to plead guilty!"

31

The courtroom fell absolutely silent. You could have heard a pin drop, but it was Raine's heart that was doing the dropping.

"Oh, Mike," he said under his breath. "You didn't need to do that."

But it was too late. Hawkins may have addressed the judge, but everyone in the courtroom heard him, including the jury. Especially the jury.

Judge Wooten's expression of shock slowly gave way to another one of those broad, toothy smiles. "You folks sure know how to have fun up here, don't you? Bailiff, please escort the jury to the jury room. I think I need to talk with the lawyers for a bit."

Raine walked around to stand next to his client. "What are you doing, Mike?" He shook his head at him. "I had it under control."

Hawkins shook his head. "It's okay, Dan. I know what I'm doing."

Once the door to the jury room closed, Judge Wooten

leaned forward, still grinning in disbelief. "Mr. Raine, I take it you are as surprised by this turn of events as everyone else?"

"I am, Your Honor," Raine confirmed. "I'm going to need some time to speak with my client."

"And go over the guilty plea form," Alexander added, his pleasure poorly concealed.

"I think we're all going to need a little time to decide what to do with this," Judge Wooten said.

"I don't need any time," Hawkins spoke up. "I'm ready to plead guilty to the first-degree murder of Lydia Szabo. I can fill out the guilty plea form myself. I'm very familiar with it."

"I'm sure you are," Wooten chuckled, "but that doesn't mean I'm going to let you plead guilty without consulting with your lawyer first. It sounds like that consultation has not happened yet."

"I don't need—" Hawkins tried, but Judge Wooten cut him off.

"Judge Hawkins, please." Wooten raised his voice just enough to remind everyone he was still in charge. "This is my courtroom. I will run it as I see fit. And I do not see fit to allow a man to enter a surprise guilty plea to the crime of murder in the first degree without taking at least some time to consider how we suddenly arrived at this position." He turned to Raine. "How much time do you need to talk to your client, Mr. Raine?"

"I'm still processing what just happened and why," Raine answered. "It will take me some time. I think we should adjourn until next week."

"Next week?" Alexander piped in. "With all due respect, Your Honor, the State has an interest in the outcome of this case as well. The defendant has just expressed, and very unequivocally, that he is guilty and wants to plead guilty. He has a right to do that, and we should not countenance a situation where his lawyer browbeats him out of doing what he just told the judge, jurors, and everyone else that he wants to do. I would suggest we recess for one hour, then reconvene with the intent to accept the defendant's guilty plea."

"Your Honor," Raine began to protest, but the judge raised a hand at him.

"We will not reconvene in one hour," Judge Wooten said, "but neither will we adjourn for an entire week. I will adjourn the case for one day. We will reconvene at nine o'clock tomorrow morning. If Judge Hawkins still wishes to plead guilty, then we will accommodate that, and the trial will be over. If he has a change of mind, his outburst may be sufficient motivation for the parties to expedite the remainder of the trial and allow the jury to return the verdict I think we would all now expect."

Judge Wooten raised his gavel to adjourn, but Alexander chimed in one last time.

"Your Honor, before we adjourn," he said, "the State would move to raise the defendant's bail. There has been a significant change in circumstances. He is about to be convicted, thanks to his own action. Should he have a change of heart, tonight would be his last chance to flee. The Court should not allow that to be even remotely possible."

Judge Wooten frowned thoughtfully. "What say you, Mr. Raine?"

Raine shook his head and looked to Hawkins. "What do you suggest I argue, Mike?"

Hawkins looked up at the judge and extended his wrists. "I'm ready to go into custody, Your Honor. There's no sense in delaying it."

"So be it," Judge Wooten ruled. "Bailiff, call a marshal and have the defendant taken into custody. Bail will be raised to five million, and the original bail shall be returned to whoever posted it."

Raine found small comfort that Yu would be happy to get his money back.

When the marshal arrived to remand Hawkins into custody, Raine asked for a conference room where they could talk before Hawkins was taken to the jail and went through the hours-long booking process. Raine didn't have hours to waste. Fortunately, the judge agreed, and a few minutes later, Raine and Hawkins were staring at each other through bulletproof glass, their voices audible only because of the circle of small holes drilled through the partition.

"I'm sorry, Dan," Hawkins spoke first. "I don't expect you to understand."

Raine sighed. "I have kids. I understand. You think you're protecting Trevor."

"That's what fathers do," Hawkins offered in explanation.

Raine looked at his watch. "Okay. That's it then. I have just under twenty-two hours."

"Twenty-two hours?" Hawkins questioned. "For what?"

"To prove Emil Szabo murdered Lydia," Raine answered. "I'm not done saving you from a life in prison. Because that's what friends do."

32

R aine had too many people to talk to and not enough time to do it. But there was an order to it. First had to be Trevor and Cindy, who were waiting for him in the hallway when he finished talking with Hawkins.

"Dan!" Cindy called out. "What just happened? Trevor said Mike pleaded guilty. Why would he do that? You were supposed to win the case, not tell him to plead guilty."

"I can assure you that I did not tell him to plead guilty," Raine responded. "I told him something that made him think it was the right thing to do. He's wrong. And I have very little time to fix this."

"What did you say?" Cindy demanded.

But Raine shook his head. "I can't say. For a lot of reasons. Attorney-client privilege for one. For another, the trial isn't over, despite what Mike just did. Trevor isn't done testifying. Everything is frozen until tomorrow morning at nine. I have to go."

"Dan." Cindy reached out and grabbed his arm. "You were supposed to win this."

Raine covered her hand with his. "I know. I'm not done trying."

THE NEXT PERSON Raine needed to talk to would be found in the West Precinct, Queen Sector 2. Luckily, it was day shift, and Sokolowski was finishing another speeding ticket when Raine tracked him down.

"Sokolowski!" he called out after parking his car behind Sokolowski's cruiser. "Get out of your car!"

Sokolowski pushed open the car door and stood up. He stared hard at Raine and hovered his hand over his sidearm.

"Don't worry, Sokolowski," Raine shouted at him, "I'm not going to attack you. I have a message for your boss. Not your sergeant. Your other boss. Szabo. Tell him to meet me at the Peony Spa after closing tonight. I know you know where that is."

Sokolowski narrowed his eyes at Raine. "Why should he?"

"Because Hawkins is going to plead guilty first thing tomorrow morning," Raine answered. "And I have the money Trevor owes him. All of it. I'll give it to him in exchange for a promise that Hawkins will be safe in prison. No orders to kill him. I want to make a deal with Szabo, but it needs to be face-to-face. Tell him to be there if he wants his money."

Sokolowski didn't answer, but Raine knew he'd pass on the message. Just like he knew Sokolowski would show up at the spa too.

"Rebecca Sommers, Executive Realtor," Sommers answered her phone.

"Rebecca. It's Dan."

"I know," Sommers answered. "Your name comes up on my screen when you call. What's going on? How's the trial going?"

"About as badly as it could," Raine answered. "Hawkins announced to God, the jury, and everyone that he was guilty. He's scheduled to plead guilty first thing tomorrow morning."

"Is he guilty?" Sommers asked.

"No," Raine answered. "He thinks he's protecting his son. He's wrong. And I have one chance to fix this before it's too late."

"And you need my help," Sommers knew. "Tell me when and where."

"Eight o'clock tonight. That same parking lot across the street from the Peony Spa," Raine answered. "I need eyes and ears. Especially if things go wrong."

"What are the odds of things going wrong?"

Raine laughed darkly. "A lot higher than things going right."

RAINE WALKED into Screaming Eagle Bail Bonds and directly to Edna's desk.

"Mr. Raine." She remembered him. "I'm afraid Mr. Yu isn't here right now."

"That's okay," Raine replied. "I just came by with a message for him and a question for you."

Edna cocked her head at him. "What are they?"

"The message for Sebastian is that he's about to get his money back," Raine answered. "And my question for you is, do you still want to do something exciting?"

THE FINAL PERSON Raine needed to talk to was the woman who saved his life the last time he went to the Peony Spa. He went there in person. It was an in-person conversation.

"Welcome to Peony Spa," she said at the sound of the front door opening. Then she looked up. "You! What are you doing here? You could get us both killed."

"There's still time for that," Raine replied. "But no time to argue. I know you're an undercover cop, and I need your help. Tonight. Here."

The woman's mouth dropped open. Her eyes darted all around the lobby. "I-I don't know what you're talking about."

Raine shook his head. "There's no time for that. I know, but Szabo doesn't. I can change that with a phone call, so unless you want me to undo what Detective Kevin Ewing said was six months of work, I need you to drop the act and help me."

The woman glanced around the business again. "What do you want me to do?"

"It's simple," Raine assured her. "I need a cop to listen in on a little conversation I'm going to have with Mr. Szabo here after closing. I need a witness when he confesses to murdering his daughter."

The woman shook her head. "That probably won't work. If you're going to confront him, he'll have his son and other goons with him. When they talk crime, they never do it in English. Do you speak Hungarian?"

"No," Raine conceded. "But I know a gal."

33

The Peony Spa closed at 8:00 p.m. Raine and Edna arrived at 7:57 and waited in his car at the far end of the parking lot. Sommers was already parked across the street. A light rain had arrived with the sunset.

"Do you understand the plan?" Raine asked Edna as the hour approached.

She nodded, the confidence she naturally radiated not faded in the slightest. "I let you do the talking. I do the listening."

"Exactly," Raine confirmed.

At 8:00 exactly, the neon 'OPEN' sign in the front window turned off. Raine hoped the cop on the inside knew where she could observe from without being seen.

A minute later, the cop on the outside arrived, brazenly in his marked patrol car. Sokolowski pulled himself out of his car, the rain bouncing off his dark blue polyester jumpsuit, and glared around menacingly.

Two minutes later, the car all of them had been waiting for arrived. A black Aston Martin sedan. It parked directly in front of the spa. Emil Szabo stepped out of the passenger side. Alexei Szabo emerged from the driver's seat.

"Damn," Raine hissed under his breath. He wasn't surprised Alexei was there, but he let himself be disappointed that the plan would be more difficult to pull off than if Szabo had elected to arrive with a couple of generic stooges. Alexei would do anything to prove his loyalty to his father. Raine was glad he'd brought his handgun, hidden in its holster under his suit coat.

"What's wrong?" Edna asked. She too was wearing a suit coat, pulled over the blouse and skirt she'd worn to work that morning.

"Nothing I didn't anticipate," Raine answered. He reached for the door handle. "Come on. Let's do this."

They both stepped out into the rain and walked over to where Szabo, Szabo, and Sokolowski were standing on the sidewalk in front of the restaurant.

"Mr. Raine," Emil Szabo greeted him with a nod. "I understand you have a business proposition for me. I'm sorry to hear your court case is not going well."

Raine shrugged. "At least it will be over tomorrow. This is just a loose thread I need to tie off before I can get back to my other cases."

"Of course," Szabo replied. He nodded toward Edna. "And who is this lovely young lady?"

"She's with my," he hesitated, "let's say, 'bank'. She's here to confirm the details of the transaction and then execute it. As you perhaps understand, this payment needs to come through a nontraditional source."

Szabo nodded. "I can understand that." He looked toward the entrance. "Shall we take this inside? I'd rather not do business in the rain. Or be seen out here with this particular collection of people."

Raine had no objection to that. To the contrary, he was counting on it. He gestured toward the door. "After you."

They all filed inside the spa. Raine could imagine Sommers cursing across the street. But he needed eyes on the outside too.

Once inside, Szabo stopped them short of going past the lobby. "I think we can do this here," he directed. "Officer Sokolowski told me you have a proposal. I'd like to hear it from you."

Raine nodded. "It's simple. Tomorrow morning, Judge Hawkins is going to plead guilty to the murder of your daughter. We both know he didn't do it, but that is irrelevant now."

"Let me stop you right there." Szabo raised a hand at Raine. "I know no such thing. I very much hold Hawkins and his entire family responsible for the death of my daughter."

Raine cocked his head at Szabo. "Directly? Or more generally, because they turned her against you and she threatened to expose the human trafficking operation if you didn't leave Trevor alone?"

Szabo wasn't a man prone to smiling, but he managed something between a grimace and a sneer. "Perhaps both. Certainly the latter, but also the former. The police and prosecutor certainly think he did it."

"That doesn't mean anything," Raine responded. He pointed at Sokolowski. "Cops are stupid. Prosecutors are lazy."

Sokolowski took an angry step toward Raine, but Szabo extended an arm to stop him.

"You seem new to this sort of transaction, Mr. Raine," Szabo said. "It's not conducive to business to antagonize the other side."

"That hasn't always been my experience," Raine returned. "One of the first things I do in a trial is try to throw off my opponent."

"This isn't a courtroom, Mr. Raine," Szabo responded, "and I am not some lazy prosecutor. You won't get in my head, I assure you."

"I'm already in Sokolowski's," Raine noted. He nodded to Alexei. "But not your son's. He must take after you." He ran a hand down the side of his own face. "It's hard to tell if there's a family resemblance, but he has your stoicism. Nice to see you again, by the way, Alexei. Maybe when this is over, we can pick up where we left off, only my hands aren't tied behind my back."

Alexei grinned. "Gladly."

Szabo clicked his tongue. "Did you really come here just to insult my child? I thought you were smarter than that."

"I am," Raine assured him. "Please accept my apologies. I just want to settle Trevor's debt and let my friend go off to prison without having to worry about getting a shiv in his back on your orders. It's just..." He shook his head. "Why did you kill Lydia? Couldn't you have just maimed her like you did your son?"

"Are you accusing me of murdering my own daughter?" Szabo asked.

"Didn't you?" Raine asked. "I don't care what the valet you gave a hundred and fifty bucks to said. You were inside when she was shot. You had the motive."

Szabo stared at him, then laughed and turned to Alexei. He said something to him in Hungarian and laughed again.

Alexei laughed less but answered his father in Hungarian. They exchanged a few more sentences, then Szabo turned back to Raine. "You are mistaken, Mr. Raine. And I fear I may have been mistaken to waste my time with this meeting. If you leave here alive, it will only be so you can appear in court tomorrow and make sure Judge Hawkins pleads guilty to the murder. But I would very much like to get my money as well."

Raine raised a finger at Szabo. "Give me a moment with my banker. I need to confer with her."

Szabo frowned but he didn't refuse the request.

Raine shepherded Edna to the farthest corner, which still wasn't that far away. "What did they say?" he whispered. "Did he admit he killed her?"

Edna shook her head. "Just the opposite. They were laughing because you still hadn't figured out who really pulled the trigger."

Raine considered the timeline again. The valet didn't lie. The cop did. "Sokolowski."

Edna nodded. "Yeah. But on the old man's orders. He called Szabo after he overheard Lydia say she was going to tell you about the human trafficking. I don't know if that matters."

It mattered. It would make Szabo an accomplice, and accomplices were guilty of the same crime as the person who pulled the trigger. But Raine didn't think that person was Sokolowski.

Raine turned and strode back to his opponents. He stepped right up to Sokolowski and examined his government-issue uniform with its cheap plastic buttons. Sure enough, the one that would have closed his collar was missing.

Sokolowski shoved him away. "What are you doing?"

"Confirming you scrambled out the window after you chickened out of killing Lydia Szabo," Raine answered. He turned to Szabo. "You came to the fundraiser to confront Lydia, but when she refused to keep her mouth shut, you left —and ordered Sokolowski to kill her."

Szabo stared stone-faced at Raine. That was all the confirmation Raine needed.

"Too bad Sokolowski didn't shoot her," Raine pressed ahead. "He didn't have the guts. But he took your money when someone else did it."

"What are you talking about?" Sokolowski demanded. "How could you know that?"

"Wrong gun," Raine answered. "She was shot with Hawkins's gun, not yours."

Szabo's face contorted into an angry scowl. "Is that true?" he demanded of the cop. "Did you lie to me?"

"No!" Sokolowski insisted. "I-I knew about Hawkins's gun, too. I specifically asked him about it so I wouldn't have to use a firearm that could be traced back to me. To you."

"But you still didn't do it," Raine decided to press his advantage. Sokolowski was rattled. Szabo was doubtful. And they were focused on each other instead of him and Edna. "What happened? Did she start crying? Did you hear someone coming?"

"No, no!" Sokolowski called out. "I used that gun. I swear. And then I left before anyone came in. I swear to God."

"There wouldn't have been time to get out the window after the shot," Raine said. He pointed at Sokolowski's collar. "And you definitely went out the window. Your missing uniform button is already in evidence. No, you lost your nerve when you heard someone coming and fled out the window. Whoever actually pulled the trigger would only have had time to hide in the room and blend in with the crowd when they rushed in."

Sokolowski's mouth fell open but he had no reply.

"You fool," Szabo growled. "You had one job, and you couldn't do it."

Sokolowski threw his arms toward Raine. "What about what he said? Why not just scare her? She wouldn't really have told anyone about the human trafficking."

"Actually, she was totally going to tell me," Raine interjected. "That night, too. The only reason she didn't is because she ended up dead. No thanks to you, I might add."

Szabo looked again to Alexei, then pointed at Sokolowski and said something in Hungarian. Raine didn't need Edna to tell him it meant, 'Kill him.'

Alexei pulled a handgun out of his coat and pointed it at Sokolowski's head.

Two gunshots rang out almost simultaneously.

Sokolowski dropped to the ground, a gunshot wound in the center of his forehead. Alexei Szabo followed, blood pouring out of the bullet hole in his temple.

All remaining eyes turned to the woman standing in the doorway to the back of the spa, pointing her service weapon at Szabo.

"Yvonne?" he questioned.

"Melissa," she corrected. "Detective Melissa Chae. And you're under arrest."

Raine looked to Edna. She had a small spatter of blood across her white silk blouse. Raine wondered which of the dead men had supplied it.

"You were right." Edna looked up at him with wide eyes. "That was exciting."

34

Court the next morning did not go the way anyone involved in the trial had expected when they went home the day before. Anyone but Raine, and even he was a little surprised at how it had turned out.

Raine got there early, but he wasn't alone. Hawkins was already in the courtroom, seated at the defense table, dressed in a suit but still handcuffed, with two jail guards standing within lunging distance behind him.

"Did you do it?" Hawkins asked as soon as Raine reached him. "Did you get Szabo to confess to murdering Lydia?"

Raine thought for a moment. "Close enough."

Hawkins frowned at him. "What does that mean?"

Raine raised a finger to his lips, then pointed at Alexander, who sauntered into the courtroom just then, grinning and obviously ready to celebrate another win. Instead, he was confronted by Detectives Kevin Ewing and Melissa Chae.

"You need to dismiss the case, John," Ewing got right to it.

"What?" Alexander croaked. "Why in the world would I do that? He's going to plead guilty."

"No, he's not," Raine spoke up from the defense table. "Change in circumstances."

Alexander frowned deeply. "What is everyone talking about? What is going on?"

So, Chae explained it all. The spa. The human trafficking. The months-long undercover operation. The confrontation that previous night. The confession, even if it was in Hungarian. "Judge Hawkins didn't murder Lydia Szabo."

Further explanation was cut short by the call of the bailiff. "All rise! The King County Superior Court is now in session, the Honorable Frank Wooten, visiting judge, presiding."

Judge Wooten emerged from his borrowed chambers with a spring in his step and a grin on his weathered face. "Good morning, everyone. I'm eager to learn what we're doing this morning."

He sat down and bade everyone else to do the same. "Mr. Raine, how does your client wish to proceed today?"

Raine stood up to address the Court. "Your Honor, I believe Mr. Alexander has a motion."

"Is that right?" Wooten's smile broadened. He turned to Alexander. "And, pray tell, what is your motion, Mr. Alexander? Does the State need additional time to look into how to proceed under these unusual circumstances?"

Raine looked at Alexander. Alexander looked at Ewing. Ewing looked to Chae. And Chae looked back at Alexander.

"No, Your Honor," Alexander answered. "The State moves to dismiss the case against Judge Hawkins."

Wooten's thick eyebrows shot up, but the grin didn't drain fully away from his face. "Dismiss?"

"Yes, Your Honor," Alexander confirmed.

Wooten leaned forward to stare directly at Alexander. "You are moving to dismiss a first-degree murder charge after the defendant said in open court that he's guilty?"

"Actually, Your Honor," Raine interjected, "Judge Hawkins said he wanted to plead guilty. He never said he was guilty."

Judge Wooten chuckled at that. "I suppose that is a distinction, counselor." He turned back to Alexander. "I see two people standing next to you, one of whom I recognize as the lead detective in this case. Am I correct to infer the other person is also a law enforcement officer?"

"Yes, Your Honor," Alexander confirmed.

"And I take it they have brought you new information which makes you believe you should dismiss the case," Wooten continued. "Is that correct?"

"That is correct, Your Honor," Alexander admitted with a sigh.

Judge Wooten nodded thoughtfully. His usual grin was replaced by an expression of seriousness, even solemnity. "Mr. Alexander."

"Yes, Your Honor?"

"Would you say that the interests of justice dictate that this case should be dismissed?"

Alexander hesitated, but only for a moment. "Yes, Your Honor, I would."

Judge Wooten nodded. "Well, this has certainly been an interesting case. Definitely worth the time and trouble to come up to Seattle." He looked down at the parties. "Judge Hawkins, I will look forward to seeing you again under better circumstances. Mr. Raine, you have my congratulations. And, Mr. Alexander, your motion is granted." He banged his gavel one last time. "Case dismissed."

EPILOGUE

A few weeks after the dismissal, Raine and Sawyer were invited to a celebratory dinner at the Hawkins home. Trevor had found a job and was finally going to move out, so they had two things to celebrate. Hawkins grilled steaks again. Raine brought another bottle of 10-year-old bourbon.

It was a dinner of thanks and relief, stories and jokes, reflection and mourning, community and healing. And after that, there were dishes to do. Trevor stepped up and said he would do them. Hawkins insisted on helping. Sawyer offered to supervise their efforts.

Raine and Cindy stepped on the back patio to breathe in the night air and admire the stars.

"Thank you again, Dan." Cindy patted him on the shoulder. "I knew you'd win the case."

Raine smiled at that. "You had a lot of confidence in me. Probably too much. But I'm glad it all worked out in the end."

"It sure did," Cindy agreed.

After a moment, and without looking at her, Raine said, "Ask me a legal question."

"What?" Cindy laughed at the suggestion.

"Ask me a legal question," Raine repeated. "Anything. It doesn't matter."

"Um, okay." Cindy took a moment to consider. "What's the sentence for manslaughter?"

Raine had to smile at the question. "With no priors, the sentence for manslaughter in the first degree is about seven years. For second-degree manslaughter, it's about two-and-a-half."

"Good." Cindy nodded. "Now I know that."

"And now you and I have an attorney-client relationship," Raine added. "Anything you say to me is confidential. I can't tell anyone. Not even Mike. Not Trevor. And certainly not the police."

Cindy's grin drained away. She locked her eyes on her new attorney.

"Was it an accident?" Raine asked. "I know you walked in on Lydia in Mike's study. I know Sokolowski had just bailed out of the window. Did the idiot take Mike's gun out of the drawer but then leave it on the desk? He said he knew the gun was there, but I know he didn't shoot it."

Cindy didn't say anything, so Raine continued.

"Did you think Lydia was going to use it on you, so you grabbed it first? Have you ever even fired a gun? Did you flinch? It's not murder if it was an accident. It's manslaughter. It sounds like you already knew that."

Again, no reply from Cindy.

"Even if it was murder," Raine continued, "I could never tell anyone. Attorney-client privilege, remember? I know Mike didn't do it. Trevor wouldn't have been smart enough to wipe off the fingerprints. That leaves you. I just want to know the truth, Cindy, even if the truth stops at me."

Cindy stared at Raine for the longest time. He had said his piece. He waited for her to answer, eyes on the stars shimmering above them.

"The truth?" Cindy asked finally. "You want to know the truth?"

Raine turned to her, a bit surprised to find her eyes waiting to lock onto his. "Yes."

"The truth is that it was an accident," Cindy admitted. "The truth is that she looked at the gun first, but I was closer. The truth is that she was scared to death because of what had just happened to her, but I mistook her agitation for something dangerous."

Cindy lowered her head and sighed deeply. "I never meant to pull the trigger. I didn't even realize I had until it was too late. I thought if I put the gun down on the floor next to her, people might think it was a suicide. I never expected Mike to run in and pick up the gun like the big, dumb, lovable fool he is. The truth is, I was too scared to say anything. I needed you to win the case."

"What if I'd lost?" Raine asked. "Would you have confessed then?"

Cindy looked up at the stars again. "I'd like to think I would have," she answered, "but I don't know for certain. Thank you for winning the case, Dan. I knew I could count on you."

WE HOPE YOU ENJOYED THIS BOOK

If you could spend a moment to write an honest review on Amazon, no matter how short, we would be extremely grateful. They really do help readers discover new authors.

ALSO BY STEPHEN PENNER

Rain City Legal Thriller Series

Burden of Proof

Trial By Jury

The Survival Rule

Double Jeopardy

Prime Suspects

Body of Evidence

Judge and Jury

The Rain City Box Set (Books 1 - 4)

Made in United States
Troutdale, OR
12/02/2025